PRAISE FOR THE NOVELS OF ERICA ORLOFF

MAFIA CHIC

"The author of *Diary of a Blues Goddess* and *Divas Don't Fake It* scores again with a charming heroine and a winsome tale."
—*Booklist*

SPANISH DISCO

"Cassie is refreshingly free of the self-doubt that afflicts most of her peers."
—*Publishers Weekly*

"This fast-paced and funny novel has a great premise and some interesting twists…"
—*Romantic Times*

DIARY OF A BLUES GODDESS

"With a luscious atmosphere and a lively, playful tone, Orloff's novel is a perfect read for a hot summer night."
—*Booklist*

THE ROOFER

"Orloff's characters are wonderful, most particulary Ava, who is resilient enough to take a chance on love."
—*Romantic Times*

"*The Roofer* is a fantastic novel…fans of urban noir romances will appreciate the contrast between glitter and grim and hopelessness and love in a deep, offbeat tale…."
—Harriet Klausner

Do They Wear High Heels in Heaven?

Erica Orloff

**RED
DRESS
INK**
TM

DO THEY WEAR HIGH HEELS IN HEAVEN?

A Red Dress Ink novel

ISBN 0-373-89535-6

© 2005 by Erica Orloff.

www.RedDressInk.com

Printed in U.S.A.

To all survivors

Acknowledgments

As always, I thank my agent, Jay Poynor, who has felt
an affinity for this book from Day One.

To my brilliant editor, Margaret Marbury, for her insights
and her friendship; the cover design team at Red Dress Ink;
Dianne Moggy; Isabel Swift; Donna Hayes—an absolutely
empowering team at my wonderful publisher.

To J.B., C.C., M.K.N., and all survivors of cancer I know,
as well as all the ones I don't.

To Writer's Cramp—Pam, Gina and Jon—without the push to
"bring pages" every two weeks, I am certain I would go six
months without producing a lousy paragraph.

To my wonderful family and friends: Maryanne, Walter, Stacey,
Jessica, Pam, Kathy J., Kathy L., Kerri, Gloria, Joey, Alexa,
Nicholas and Isabella. And finally, to J.D. for understanding
that this writer was never meant to cook,
visit a grocery store, or keep her mouth shut.

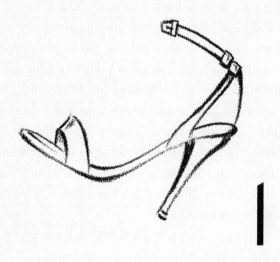

Lily

My phone rang, and I reached a hand out into the blackness and fumbled for the receiver.

My best friend's voice spoke, singsong. "Is this the decrepit old hag?"

I groaned and looked at the clock on my nightstand. "Payback's a bitch, Michael. Just remember that."

"Happy birthday, ancient troll."

"It's five-thirty in the morning."

"But you know the tradition."

Ever since Michael and I discovered, nearly twenty years ago, that our birthdays fell a week apart, the tradition has been to be the first person to wish the other a happy birthday. Somehow, with Michael's latent gay frat-boy sensibility, this has disintegrated into phone

calls at 5:00 a.m. and relentless teasing and Over The
Hill black balloons. Rather than maintaining my dignity, of course, I have gone birthday for birthday with
him, each of us escalating the idiocy. By the time we're
ninety, I am sure he will be hiding my false teeth, and
I will be sending buff male strip-o-grams—like the
"cops" who yank their tear-away pants off—to the
nursing home. If I hadn't answered the phone, he would
have let himself into my house with his key and likely
dumped ice water on my head. It's been done. The year
I turned twenty-seven.

"Like I said, my bestest friend, payback's a bitch." I
smiled despite myself. "And I live for revenge."

"We'll see."

"We will indeed."

"And how does it feel…being the big 4—"

"*Don't* say it."

"Four-oh. I said it."

"Fuck you, Michael," I laughed. Then I hung up on
him. Three seconds later my phone rang again.

"Forty. Forty. Forty. Forty."

"Fuck you. Fuck you. Fuck you. Fuck you." I hung
up on him again. And once again it rang. "Shut up!" I
snapped into the phone before he could speak.

"Now, Lily…I mean it sincerely. Because you're so
much *older* than I am, you need to tell me how it *feels*
to be so hideously ancient."

"First of all, I'm thirty-five. Second, you'll know how
it feels soon enough. In one week, specifically."

He hooted into the phone. "I've *seen* your driver's li-

cense. Thirty-five. This is the big one, my dear old—
and I do mean old—friend. The one you've been fret-
ting about since you *actually* turned thirty-five. Enjoy the
day."

I let out a half laugh and hung up the phone, then
rolled over and tried to fall back to sleep. It was Saturday. Ever since my son Noah discovered PlayStation *and*
grew tall enough to get his own apple juice from the
fridge—albeit while leaving sticky juice residue on the
kitchen counter—I have rediscovered the joy of sleeping until eight-thirty. Saturday has taken on a quasi-re-
ligious status. It is sacred. There was a time, of course,
P.K. (prekids), P.M.A.D (premarriage and atomic divorce), when I would think nothing of staying over at
a lover's apartment, sleeping in, having lazy Saturday
sex, showering together, and then heading off to a late
brunch—which would usually include spicy Bloody
Marys and reading the *Times*—before going back to the
apartment for more lazy Saturday sex…and then a nap.
I let out a mostly silent groan at the thought. Yet another reminder I am no longer twenty. Well, that and
breasts that have gone through a combined total of
nearly two and a half years of breastfeeding. They used
to be perky enough to go braless. No more.

I rolled over in bed. It sucks being a grown-up. It also
used to be that I could easily fall back to sleep once
woken. Mothers lose that ability, and thanks to Michael,
I was up for the day. I climbed out of bed and padded
into the bathroom. I shut the door and flicked on the
light. Squinting as my eyes adjusted to the brightness, I

surveyed my body in the full-length mirror—and suddenly felt something akin to panic.

Racing out of the bathroom, I grabbed my phone and dialed Michael. He answered on the first ring. Obviously he hadn't gone back to bed either—if he even had *gone* to bed. He had no kids. He still got to do things like that.

"Yeah?"

"It's the end of life as we know it."

"I know. You're forty. I can hear your hips creaking."

"No. Worse."

"What can be worse than that?"

"I just discovered my first gray pubic hair."

"Might as well commit suicide. Can you dye down there?"

"I don't know. I never gave it a thought. Just like I never gave it a thought that one day I might not *want* a tattoo of a pink flamingo on my ass. You do know asses sag, don't you?"

"Yours is still firm."

"I know. But I'm picturing seventy-year-old flamingo-ass. Like I'm now picturing completely gray granny pubic hair. I think I need to get drunk today."

"Which is why I'll be there in a matter of thirty minutes, with the fixings for Bloody Marys and a box of Krispy Kremes."

"I'm going to pluck it."

"Good. I think you should. Then we should get drunk."

"Krispy Kremes?"

"Warm. Fresh out of the oven. Screw Atkins. Life is too short not to eat carbs."

"You know, if it wasn't for your being gay, I'd consent to your being my second husband."

"I thought you swore off marriage as a matter of principle."

"I did. But we're talking Krispy Kremes."

"See you in a few. Shower. Put on your makeup. Then tell yourself that flamingo-ass of yours is still hot."

"See you in a few."

I hung up the phone. I knew why Michael was driving over. It was the same reason he always spent my birthday with me. Because left on my own to ponder gray hair and another year, I'd wallow in self-pity for days.

As I showered, I thought about why. When I was younger, it was the concept of milestones. When I turned twenty-eight, I decided I could no longer lay claim to being in my "mid-twenties," and therefore had to say I was in my "late-twenties." And with each passing year, I felt something else slip away. Now, at forty-pretending-to-be-thirty-five, I knew that this birthday, in particular, meant the end of sex.

It's not that I thought I would never have sex again, but with aching clarity, growing older is a reminder that at some point—some line of demarcation—you will never again put on a little black dress and a pair of stilettos, walk into the room, be wanted by any man in it with a pulse, make eye contact with a tall, dark and handsome stranger and know if you wanted to bed him, you could. You cease to be a sexual being in the same way you were when you were twenty-two, when something about the very air you breathed, your scent, made you an object of desire. At forty, you can still be desired, but it requires more intimacy. More effort. When you are desired at forty, it is for the whole exhausting package—your mind, your looks, the connection of two souls. But when you're wanted at twenty-two, it's because, frankly, you're a hot lay. And with age comes wisdom that while the whole package is a more intense experience, there's still a mourning for what you once were. What you once could have just because you wanted it.

I finished showering, pulled on my silk robe, put on my makeup—deciding that Chanel red lipstick was a forty kind-of-color—blew-dry my hair and went downstairs to start the coffeemaker. I heard a car in the driveway, and went to my front door and opened it for Michael.

And there, in my robe, I was greeted by the sight of forty (I counted later) large pink plastic flamingos stuck like a hungry flock into my yard. Michael climbed out of his black Spyder convertible.

"Like 'em?" he grinned, holding a shopping bag and a box of Krispy Kremes.

"When did you do this?"

"At 3:00 a.m."

"Do you know how juvenile you are?"

"Absolutely."

"I think this is the start of a very long day."

"Baby…" He smiled at me. "You have no idea the things I've planned."

"Come on in." It was then I turned around and got a good look at my dog, Gunther, who came lumbering in from his sleeping spot in the laundry room. He was wearing a doggie T-shirt that read, My Bitch Is 40.

I rolled my eyes.

A long, long day calling for many, many Bloody Marys.

2

Michael

The CIA has nothing on Lily. Nothing. Come our birthday week, she can fuck with my mind in ways psychological torturers *wish* they could come up with. Drop her into enemy territory and the opposition will be begging for surrender.

So the night *before* my fortieth birthday, she actually pulled off a surprise party. In order to do this, she enlisted the help of the departmental chair of the English department of Hudson University, Martin Robeson. Until the moment when ol' Marty yelled "Surprise!" I hadn't even known he had a sense of humor.

That Friday morning, I heard him in his office yelling, "Damn, damn, damn!" at the top of his lungs.

I poked my head into his office, "What's up, Martin?"

In a performance worthy of Shakespeare, he passed his hand across his brow. "I have a potential professor for the opening next fall flying in from Scotland, and damn that Helen also has me scheduled to meet with the dean for dinner."

He eyed me slightly desperately. "I don't suppose you could…"

"Oh no." I held up my hands. "Most definitely not, Martin. Entertain some Scottish windbag…I don't think so."

"Please, Michael. I'm desperate. I'll owe you. Handsomely."

He is my boss. So next thing I knew, I was headed to the airport in Westchester to pick up Professor Hugh McDonnell. He, all two hundred and eighty pounds and red beard, was waiting on the curb at six o'clock. He had the loudest voice I've ever heard in my life and a brogue so thick I could barely understand him. He also apparently believed in punctuating any sentence with the slightest bit of emotion with a slap on the back.

"Marty tells me you teach Milton," Professor McDonnell said, his voice rising and falling in a lilting way.

"I do."

"Ahh yes, he of the many sins…. Sin's a wonderful thing, is it not? Rich fodder for teaching literature."

"Sure, sure." I nodded, trying to keep my eyes on the road.

"And not too bad for having a bangin' good time, eh?" His voice boomed, and he laughed, which sounded like a cross between a howl and a guttural hoot. Then he punched me in the arm.

Martin had promised the good professor dinner at a place down on the water in Nyack, New York. So, being punched in the arm every few minutes, I headed to the Wharfside restaurant, walked in and was bombarded with "Surprise!" and the sight of everyone I knew—and even some I didn't—gathered for my party. At that point, Professor Hugh McDonnell nearly collapsed with laughter. He also lost his brogue. I'd been had. And Martin, uptight little anal-retentive that he is, looked very pleased that he was at last "one of the gang" and had pulled off the ultimate surprise.

And there was Lily. Front and center in a little black cocktail dress, stilettos—she was in chronic denial about her five-foot three-inch height-challenged size—and her hair and makeup perfect.

She walked over and hugged me. "Gotcha!"

"I drove all the way to the airport for nothing?"

"Don't be bitchy," she urged with a pout. "Not for nothing. For this surprise, Michael. You should see your face."

"Next year all bets are off."

"Darling, you'll never be able to top this." She turned to "Hugh." "Thanks, John. I owe you one."

He was still wiping tears from his eyes. "Classic! Classic! Oh my God, but that was fun."

Turned out Professor Hugh McDonnell was the brother-in-law of one of Lily's coworkers at the paper—and an actor from Manhattan.

Tara and Noah, Lily's kids, were there, along with everyone from the English Department at Hudson University, Lily's friends from the paper, my book editor and his assistant, my literary agent, Charlie, even my high school buddy, Zack, who'd flown in from St. Louis for the occasion. By nine o'clock I was blind drunk, and I recall lots of sloppy kissing, many hugs, and I believe I repeated the expression, "I love you guys" about a hundred times, each one successively more effusive.

After the party, Lily decided I was in no condition to drive home, so she—helped by the burly imposter Scotsman—piled me into her minivan and drove me to her house. The kids had been brought home earlier by her neighbor, Connie, who has yet to accept I am gay and has tried to seduce me too many times to count.

I stumbled up the stairs, after nearly tripping over Gunther, who was lying in the foyer. I went into the master bedroom and flopped onto Lily's bed and flicked on the television. She brought me a glass of water and changed into her pajamas, then went to each of the kids' bedrooms and checked on them. She came back into her bedroom and lay down next to me on top of her goosedown comforter.

"That went well, don't you think?"

"Yeah…. Thanks."

"I got you so good." She poked me, smiling.

"Yes, you did." I was determined to stay awake until I sobered up a bit. Hate bed spins.

"Were you surprised?"

"You just said you got me good."

"I know, but I'm fishing for compliments on what a great party it was."

"It was a brilliant party."

"You're forty, you know. It's after midnight."

Forty.

Actually, part of the reason I drank so much was the sight of Lily and the kids, front and center. I never had, being gay, that dream of marriage and a family and two-point-three kids and a dog. No picket fence. Chintz sofa. None of it. I never expected that to be part of the deal—not for me. Those were the cards dealt me, and I never bitched about them. But turning forty…maybe, just a little part of me wanted that. The two-point-three kids thing. Not the dog. Gunther is enough dog on a part-time basis. He snores—and slobbers. I like my gold-fish. Glenda the goldfish has lived for four years, which I consider some sort of record.

"You didn't answer me, Michael. How does it feel?"

"You should know. You turned forty last week—gray pubic hair and panic is what I recall."

"Don't change the subject."

"It feels…weird…. I keep thinking about death."

"God, you're morbid. I keep thinking about sex. Lack of it."

"I don't have that problem."

"No, you don't. You have your little boy toys."

"Feels…a little empty at forty."

"Put on Conan O'Brien."

I clicked over and took a sip of water. Less spins, slightly queasy.

"You're lucky, you know. Having kids and all that."

Lily leaned up on one elbow. "I know. But you have them, too. By proxy."

"Yes, by gay proxy."

"Now if I could only have as much sex as you by proxy."

"Well, you could, but my kind isn't what you're really dying to have."

"No. I suppose not." She yawned. "God, you're an old hag."

"Old fag."

"That, too."

"Thanks again, Lily. It was fabulous. Loved the chicken satay."

"Mmm. Me, too. Though the crew from the English department was hogging them. Don't they feed you people?"

"No. They keep us locked up in the ivory tower on bread and water."

"'Night, Michael."

She rolled over and got comfortable, and soon her eyelids grew heavy. I sipped some more water.

We were like an old married couple. Minus the sex.

Though, given what my over-forty married friends say about their sex lives, maybe we had it right. Most of my over-forty married friends say they never do it anymore. Too tired. Too busy. Too apathetic. God, what happened to our wild years?

3

When Did I Become My Mother?
by Lily Waters

Every woman has the moment when she becomes her mother. The time comes in an instant of shock and awe. Real shock and awe—not the Donald Rumsfeld variety.

My daughter, Tara, has never missed an opportunity in the years since she turned twelve to point out to me that I ceased to be cool the moment I had to buy my first box of Nice 'n Easy to cover my gray. For four years now, she has pointed out I no longer wear cool clothes, listen to cool music or have the cool lingo down. Only cool's not cool anymore anyway. It's *hot*.

I have refused to believe her, of course. I *am* cool. Hot. Whatever. I still like rock and roll blasting from my stereo. All right, no self-respecting cool person would drive a minivan with juice stains on the seats and a plethora of baseball gear in the back, including cleats with mud still clinging to them, but I still roll down all the windows and sing at the top of my lungs. I like to drive fast down the hills of my hometown feeling the wind whip my hair around. I let my dog sit in the front seat. I wear Abercrombie jeans. I still have three earrings in my left ear and four in my right. I no longer wear big 1980s hoops—but I notice they're "in" again, proving my grandmother right: If you hold onto things long enough, they'll come back in style again. I wonder if that holds true for leg warmers and Pet Rocks.

I also have another "cool" thing that drove my late mother insane. I have a tattoo.

But when Tara asked me yesterday if she could get a tattoo of a soccer ball on her left shoulder, I answered with a fast, "Over my dead body!"

"Why?"

"Because…you could hate soccer four years from now and then you'll be stuck with this stupid ball on your shoulder."

"So?"

"Every time you want to wear a strapless dress, it'll show."

"That's the whole idea, Mom."

"You could get hepatitis."

"I'll go to a good place, Mom."

"There's no such thing as a *good* tattoo parlor."

"But it's my life."

"You can't permanently mark your body until you're eighteen. I mean it, Tara."

"*You* did," she said accusingly. "So why can't I?"

"Because I'm your mother, and I said so."

And there it was. I had turned into my mother—the most uncool, squarest, nerdiest, old-fashioned woman on the planet. Right there. Right in front of my daughter.

So I did what any self-respecting uncool woman would do.

I added, "And that's final!"

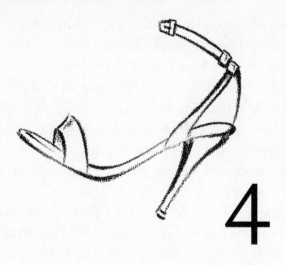

4

Lily

Monday morning
The Boomtown Rats' "I Don't Like Mondays" played
inside my head because the list of why I don't like the
first day of the workweek would, if I rattled off the rea-
sons, last longer than the song. After Bob Geldolf finished his cross between a warble and a wail, I would still
be going on.

For starters, my whole life seems to run on its own
watch, which is perpetually twenty minutes slower than
everyone else's watch. This means that I can't seem to
get myself and my two kids, Tara and Noah, out the
door in a way in which it would be possible for them

to arrive at school on time, unless we managed to somehow score a lift on the space shuttle.

Both my children have inherited my organizationally
challenged genetic defect. So, inevitably, when I get the
three of us in our minivan—which frankly I can't believe I drive—one of them will have forgotten something. Whatever this something is will not be the same
something from day to day. Monday it might be the
lunchbox on the counter for Noah, Tuesday Tara's high
school science report, Wednesday a permission slip in
which I promise not to sue the school if they manage
to lose Noah in the gorilla exhibit at the Bronx Zoo,
Thursday…well, often it's not them and *I* actually forget something, like my wallet. Friday I am so sick of the
whole morning process that I just want to declare it a
day to play hooky. Of course, going back to the "I was
so much cooler before I had kids" thing, I *was* actually
the type of kid who played hooky. Often. But now that
I am semiresponsible—to go along with my semisan-
ity—I can't very well encourage that sort of thing.

Somehow, the universe must have figured out my
flaw—my incapability to get anywhere on time—and
gave me the gift of gab. Or at least writing. So after la-
boring as a newspaper reporter for ten years in my
hometown of Rivers Landing, when I was thirty-six I
finally landed my own biweekly column in the paper—
actually one with a sizable circulation. Between that and
a book I wrote—a humorous *Divorce Survival Guide* that
was moderately successful—and freelance writing gigs,
I manage to make a living, though the roof on my house

leaks and I have had a family of chipmunks living in my walls and can't afford the exterminator until next paycheck. And I guess I feel bad for the little guys, so maybe they can keep their home in my walls. In my somewhat ugly financial picture, I also make due with rather dismally small child support from my ex-husband, Spawn of Satan, who lives in London with his vapid Child Bride. All of this combined means I am able to work from home. Except on Mondays. On Mondays, I am required to come into the offices of the *Herald Tribune* and have a meeting with my editor, Joe Streep.

Now, with technology, this Monday meeting is archaic. E-mail me. Call me. Videoconference me. Fax me, for Christ's sake. But Joe likes a face-to-face on Mondays. Personally, I think he likes having someone to argue with. I think I am his Monday-morning pick-me-up. I get his blood moving faster than a cup of coffee. I am the human equivalent of the hair of the dog that bit him, coupled with a triple shot of espresso.

Speaking of dogs, on this particular Monday, Noah's dog, Gunther, ran away. Michael gave Gunther to us two years ago, a Heinz-57 mutt Michael bought for five dollars from a kid selling pups from a shopping cart outside the grocery store Michael frequents. And Gunther apparently resents not having a better name—or he resents something—because he will listen to Michael but ignores me as if I were a rubber toy Gunther no longer cared about. So when Gunther, aka That Damn Dog, took off that Monday, I spent thirty minutes tracking him down and arrived at the office, finally, sweating, with mud on my dress pants and shoes, and my hair deciding that windblown was going to be the look for that day.

"You're late, Waters!" Joe snarled.

"Do you know you spit when you yell?"

"You have mud on your pants."

"Your tie's ugly." It was a wide paisley one whose colors recalled a time Gunther had vomited up a plate of spaghetti he had jumped up on the table to eat. Oh, and that was another thing about Gunther. Michael's "gift"—our "cute" little pup—grew to weigh ninety-six pounds.

"I can change my tie. You're stuck with that hair."

"At least I have hair. Your head reflects the fluorescent lights." And for the record, when not windblown, my hair is actually quite lovely—long, black and shiny-straight.

"I have an assignment for you."

"The last assignment you gave me involved a color piece on what you can find at the town dump."

"This is less smelly."

"Thanks."

"I want you to squash your breasts like two pancakes—for the sake of the paper."

"Sure. And why don't we cut your dick off—for the sake of the paper."

I saw Joe bite the inside of his cheek for a minute, trying to keep up that "Mr. Perry White-crabby-editor-of-Lois-Lane-and-Clark-Kent" routine. Then he burst out laughing.

Joe is about sixty. He keeps swearing he'll retire—because of how crazy I make him some days—and he is an old-time newshound. And though his bark might scare the young reporters fresh out of school and working the obit desk, I know he is a devoted grandfather of triplet girls, born to his only daughter after she had a long struggle with infertility.

"Well," he said, wiping at a tear from laughing so hard. "I'd like to keep my dick. But your breasts…they're going off to a mammogram for Breast Cancer Awareness month. We're going to run your column with a pink box around it."

"A mammogram? I'm only thirty-five. I don't even need a baseline yet."

"Lily…you've been lying about your age for so long, I think you forget how old you really are. At the very least, you forget that *I* know how old you really are. You're forty, and you can go get your baseline for the good of the paper and women everywhere. We're even picking up the tab."

"Oh, gee, thanks."

"Just do it."

"Fine. But I draw the line at pulling a Katie Couric and getting a colonoscopy. My breasts can get smashed. My ass is off-limits."

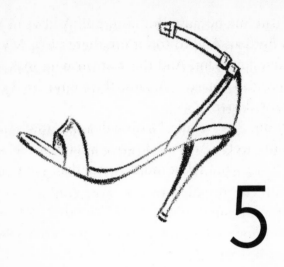

5

Michael

Only my sainted Sicilian mother could have given me a name like Michael Angelo. Nothing like stacking the cards against a kid in grade school. Actually, forget grade school, try meeting a guy in a gay bar, sticking out your hand and saying, "I'm Michael Angelo." I've heard them all. "And I'm Picasso." "And I'm the Virgin Mary." "And I'm the Pope." "And I'm the Sistine Chapel." I've sometimes slept with a guy two, three times, and he'll turn to me afterwards and say, "So what's your *real* name?"

Gay, with a moniker like mine, a mother who still believes I only need to meet the right woman, and a father who won't speak to me because apparently my being gay is a reflection on *his* manhood. Add to that people hate me because I'm beautiful. And vain. Well, it's all a burden. And to top it off, there's Lily. My best friend and confidant. And the woman who makes me supremely glad I'm gay—because there is no way I could ever live with her.

Every once in a while, Noah will ask, "How did you and Mom meet?" And we do have a "cute meet" story of our very own. I tell it much better than she does, of course.

We lived two doors down from each other in the same apartment building on the Upper East Side—she was subletting a studio—but we had never actually seen each other. I was working nights on the sports desk at one paper, and she was working days as an assistant editor for a magazine. Unbeknownst to me, however, she smelled me. Or rather, she smelled my cooking.

One night, I had called in sick, sniffling with a miserable New York winter cold, so I wasn't out prowling the bars, and I heard someone pounding on my door. Scared the hell out of me. I peered through the peephole, and in that funhouse-distortion of peephole glass I saw Lily, all five foot three inches of woman and three inches of big 1980s hair teased up high on her head, coupled with three-inch heels.

I opened the door, "Can I help you?"

She was dressed for a date, wearing a simple and elegant little black A-line and a choker of pearls. The hair didn't go with the outfit. I thought she needed something sleek, a style akin to Audrey Hepburn in *Breakfast at Tiffany's*, but I wasn't going to tell her.

"Are you the guy who's always cooking?" She spoke very fast, machine-gun rapid.

"Cooking?"

She tapped her foot impatiently. "On Sundays. Cooking… C-oo-k-ing," she said a little slower, as if I had the IQ of a doorknob. "Are you the one?"

She nervously looked down the hall, her eyes shifting from her apartment door to me. Back and forth. "Well?"

"I am."

"Yeah, well listen, I'm having a major fucking food crisis, and I need your help." She grabbed my hand and half-pulled me down the hall, where I could now, despite my cold, smell something burning.

Walking into her apartment was like walking into a five-alarm blaze. Smoke hugged the ceilings. We made our way to the tiny kitchen, where I opened a window. My eyes were tearing; my throat felt like it was closing on me.

"What the hell are you trying to cook?"

"A chicken. It's in the oven."

I pulled out a bird that had shriveled to a carcass.

"Can you help me fix it? I have a date coming over. I'll buy you a case of beer. I'll clean your apartment."

"Fix it? Fix it?" I sat down on one of her kitchen chairs and laughed. "Girl, unless you use this bird for charcoal briquettes for the *next* thing you're going to cook, there's nothing to be done with it."

"Couldn't you coat it in a sauce?"

"Sauce? If I touch this it will turn to a pile of ashes."

"I thought you called yourself a cook!" She put her hands on her hips.

"What? Honey, I don't even *know* you. I get dragged to an apartment in need of a hook and ladder truck, and *you're* picking on *me?*"

She looked at me, and then her nose crinkled up, the way I've since learned it always does when she's going to laugh. She plopped down in the other kitchen chair, and we both cracked up. The more she laughed, the more I did, until we were both holding our sides, tears rolling down our faces from smoke and laughter. Her date never showed up, and she opened the wine she had bought for him—a cheap cabernet from the grocery store…with chicken! Okay, so reds with fish and chicken may be okay today, but not in the '80s. We got drunk and told each other our life stories. From that night on, Lily and I were the best of friends.

Fast forward more years than either of us likes to confess to. Now, on Monday nights, I almost always cook dinner at her place. It gives us a chance to catch up. Otherwise, between my teaching schedule and her deadlines and everything, we'd turn into those "I haven't talked to you in six months, how have you been?" kind of friends. And since we both hate Mondays, the dinners give us something to look forward to.

Our lives have changed a lot since we first met. I'm not sure either of us pictured the journey. Does anyone? I don't think she anticipated marriage and motherhood. And divorce. I teach English, which wasn't really where I thought I'd be at this point in my life—teaching Milton and English composition to freshmen who stumble into my 8:15 class red-eyed and hungover—precisely how *I* was when I was a freshman. My dream job would be to write a sports column, but the world isn't ready for an openly gay sports columnist. Lily's dream job would be to photograph hunky firemen for one of those male pin-up calendars. The fact that nearly every picture she takes has her thumb covering the lens means nothing. Actually, come to think of it, maybe the firemen calendar is *my* dream job.

On Monday, I picked up Noah from school—he's in the second grade—and we went grocery shopping.

"One of the kids at school said gay people are disgusting."

"Hmm," I said, picking up some fresh basil, trying not to react. "And what did you say?"

"I told him it wasn't true—that *he* was disgusting. I said he was grosser than boogers."

"Well handled," I said, smiling, rubbing the top of his head. "Don't let your mother know you called someone a booger."

"She says *way* worse all the time."

"I know. But your mother is a creature who invents her own rules."

We finished our shopping and drove on to their house, a white Cape Cod with dormer windows upstairs and a sort of Currier and Ives appearance, especially with the fall leaves scattered around in golds and reds. The roof leaks—but from the outside, it really does look picture-perfect. I remember when she and the Spawn of Satan found the place. I tried to believe that they really would live happily ever after. But, like the leaky roof, sometimes there are little holes you don't notice at first. It takes a big storm to show you where the leaks are.

Noah and I started cooking dinner together. I swear the kid is a chef in the making. I even bought him a little white apron—a crisp one like you'd see on a waiter in an Italian restaurant. Noah's got a mop of unruly brown hair, a smattering of freckles across his nose and his two front teeth missing like the jack-o'-lantern we planned to carve for Halloween.

The phone rang. Tara telling us she was staying at Justin's for dinner. Justin's her first boyfriend. And he drives. A Mustang. And he's smart—a really decent guy—as well as the captain of the hockey team, which has a tremendous "coolness" factor. This whole combination makes him akin to a high-school-aged George Clooney.

"You can eat at Justin's, but you're missing your favorite—lasagna."

"Damn."

"Don't say 'damn.'"

"Okay, shit."

I rolled my eyes. "God, age fifteen."

"Sixteen in three weeks."

"Yeah, well please just fast forward to twenty-five and get all this pain-in-the-ass stuff over with."

"See you later, Uncle Michael."

"Later, sweetie."

I hung up the phone. Noah looked up from the noodles he was laying out in the pan. "Tara and Justin are gross."

"Eh…it's just first love."

"Well, I'm never going to fall in love."

"Yes, you will."

We heard the minivan pull up into the driveway. "Mom's home!" Noah shouted, hurrying to lay the noodles faster so it would be done before she walked in.

Gunther started barking like a lunatic. He's half mutt, half slobbering monster, and he ran to the front door and nearly knocked her over.

"Get down, Gunther!" Lily barked. "Sure, small paws. Ninety-six pounds later!"

After settling down the dog, she walked into the kitchen. "Hey!" She pecked my cheek hello and bent down to give Noah a hug.

"How was your day?" I asked.

"One for the record books. To start with, Gunther did this," she pointed to a smear on her pants.

"Attractive."

"Ugh…please. Today sucked. Joe was in rare form. How's this for an assignment? Go smash your breasts into pancakes for Breast Cancer Awareness Month. Tomorrow."

"Sounds like fun. More action than you've been getting lately."

"Shut the hell up."

"Mom!" Noah shouted. "Quarter!"

Lily rolled her eyes and opened her purse. She took out a dollar and put it in the curse jar, filled to the brim with money, which we spent every so often on a night of pizza and bowling. "It's been a bad day. That'll cover me for three more."

She slipped off her shoes and poured a glass of wine from the bottle that was breathing on the counter.

"How's your book going?" she asked me.

"I'm stuck."

"Why?"

I shrugged.

"You know why."

And of course I did. I was writing a novel about a baseball player at a medium-sized university. He's closeted, and when his best friend on the team discovers his secret, he outs him and the gay player is forced to leave the team in disgrace. Give up his baseball scholarship. Any hope of getting drafted. And writing it just opened up all the old wounds. Call it a novel, but it was way too close to real life. My life.

6

Curveball
An excerpt from a novel by Michael Angelo

"You're a fucking homo, aren't you?" The venom in Charlie's voice sounded murderous. "A fucking queer." His face was pale, and his normally lively green eyes looked dark.

Sam tried to laugh it off. "No…no. I'm not gay. What are you crazy?" His heart pounded, and he felt his mouth go dry as sandpaper. He looked around for someplace in their tiny dorm room to escape. Like the closet. And the irony of that was pathetic.

"Then what's this, Sam? What the hell is this?"

Sam took a step backward. From the moment he walked in the room after class and saw Charlie at his desk, Sam knew what Charlie had found. There in his spiral notebook was a page of doodles from the night before, when from too much caffeine and not enough sleep cramming for midterms, he had absentmindedly written out Charlie's name in the center of a heart with an arrow drawn through it.

"It's nothing. I don't know. I was delirious. I've been up for two days straight with this organic chemistry midterm and then practice. I'm just tired, man. Just fucking tired." Sam could hear the panic in his voice.

"Bullshit." Charlie spat and, without warning, dove for Sam, his fist connecting with Sam's right eye, and then his nose. Sam tasted the salty sweet sensation of his own blood in his mouth, and still Charlie punched him with a relentless fury. They fell against the puke-green cinderblock wall of their dorm room and landed on the floor. Sam put his arms in front of his face to defend himself.

"Stop! Stop!" he screamed. He had no choice but to fight back, and the two of them punched wildly, then struggled to their feet. They knocked over Sam's desk, and Sam's hand went sailing into the mirror, which sliced clear across his knuckles.

"Jesus Christ, Charlie, get the fuck off me!"

Charlie stopped for a moment, catching his breath. Seeing the blood covering Sam's shirt and arms, Charlie began shouting, "Fucking great. Now I could fucking get AIDS. You sick, sick fuck." Without another word, he ran from their dorm room as a small crowd gathered in the hallway. There, in the gray-carpeted hallway were Jake and his girlfriend, and next to him Tommy carrying his bong. A few others from the study lounge stood there gawking.

Sam stared at them all, then grabbed a towel and tried to staunch the bleeding in his hand.

"What happened?" Jake asked. He was the team's shortstop. Charlie and Sam were catcher and pitcher, respectively.

"Nothing. We just got into an argument."

"What happened to your hand?" Jake came over and tried to move the towel aside.

"Nothing. I said it was nothing." Sam pulled his arm away. "Show's over guys. Leave me alone, okay?"

"Suit yourself." Jake looked at him suspiciously, but in the end, they all left his room.

Sam unwrapped his hand. The gash was deep. He couldn't imagine pitching with a cut like that. But, he mused, now that Charlie had found out his secret, he wasn't sure if he could stay on the team anyway. In the world of college baseball, being queer was worse than being a rapist. It was an unforgivable sin against the *Almighty Book of Athletics*.

And falling in love with your best friend was even worse.

7

Lily

The machine whirred and moved, sounding like a cross between R2D2 and an X-ray. My right breast was stretched and pulled in ways I couldn't have imagined a half hour before. In my mind, I wasn't really thinking about the fact that I was having a mammogram, I was thinking of all the funny ways I could describe just what it is that mammogram machine *does* to your breasts.

It kneads them like dough in a bread maker.

It flattens them like…what? Like the machine was a gigantic spatula, squashing my breasts which were like so much hamburger. It paws them like that sloppy drunk and inexperienced one-night stand from freshman year of college.

"Uncomfortable?" The technician looked at me with concern. "Just let me know if it gets unbearable."

"Uncomfortable? Why no…I *love* being flattened like this. It's some sort of kinky turn-on."

She laughed. "I know. It's a pretty weird experience."

"Are you kidding? This is the most action my breasts have gotten in four months."

Which was true. Thanks to Michael playing match-maker, and the fact that, with my big mouth, I've never had problems meeting men, I never lacked for dates. I've dated older men, younger men, hunky men, bald men, chubby men, skinny men, intellectual men and goofy men. I've dated single dads—and men who at the sound of "I've got two kids" were scanning the restaurant for an exit. But most of all, I've dated baggage handlers—men with so much baggage they're like Skycaps at JFK Airport. Consequently, dates aside, I rarely make it into the bedroom. It had been a while since I met someone worth the effort of shaving my legs.

The technician, who had told me her name was Melissa, collected the films she'd taken of both breasts, and said, "I'll be back in ten minutes. I just need to check the film, and if the pictures are clear, you'll get dressed and off you go to write about this fun afternoon for your column."

"Oh joy."

She left me alone in the small room, a lead apron tied around my belly to protect my reproductive organs during the mammogram—not that I expected to need my reproductive organs again. I was pretty sure I was done having kids. Said baggage handlers meant—forget being "shave worthy"—it had been quite a while since I met anyone whose gene pool seemed like it might be an acceptable match for mine.

Twenty minutes passed, and I was still waiting, so I sat down on a stool. A short time later, Melissa was back.

"You know, there's this spot on your right breast…we'd like to do an ultrasound."

"A spot? What does it look like?"

"You know, we can't say for sure. Sometimes the ultrasound will make it clearer. We can do it right now…so grab your purse and follow me across the hall."

My breasts hadn't gotten so much action in years. Ten minutes later a new technician was rubbing an ultrasound wand—which vaguely resembles a small dildo—over and over again on my breast. Which is far less sexy than it sounds.

"Well?"

"I have to talk to one of the doctors. You just hang tight here for a little while."

"I'm not going anywhere. You've taken my clothes hostage."

While she was gone, I massaged my breast where she had been moving the ultrasound back and forth. I couldn't feel anything and assumed it was a cyst.

A short time later, I was told I could dress. The ultrasound technician walked me down the hall into the radiologist's office where I sat in a velour-covered mauve chair.

"Lily…Dr. Edie Grasso," the doctor said, extending

her hand. She looked about fifty, with frosted silver hair in a neat bob and horn-rimmed glasses. "We're going to have to do a biopsy."

I felt like the room spun around a minute, and I put my hand on her desk—maybe to confirm it was real.

"Crap."

"Yeah…I pretty much think that's what I'd say if I had to have one."

I inhaled. "This is really going to ruin the ha-ha funny column I was planning to write."

"Sorry about that. But you know, writing about this whole experience for Breast Cancer Awareness Month may help a lot of women."

"True…but first you said the b-word—biopsy. Now I have to worry about the c-word. Do you think it's cancer?"

"You know, I don't like how it looks, but we won't know anything until we biopsy it."

I swallowed hard. "I don't do sickness well. It's like the one time in my life I turn into a total wimp."

"None of us does sickness well." She smiled. "Come on…let's schedule this and get it over with. It's the not knowing that's the worst of it."

On the drive home from the women's center, I tried to decide who to tell. It could be nothing. It could be something. Either way, I was numb myself, and the idea of having to go through the *blah-blah-blah* of the mammogram, ultrasound and now the biopsy I'd scheduled, irritated me.

It reminded me of when I got divorced. Yeah, the divorce from Spawn of Satan was bad. But having to repeat the story ad nauseum was worse, I think. People I only talked to every few months or so—like my college roomie, Margot—had to be caught up to speed. This was why my answering machine no longer said, "You've reached the home of Lily, David, Tara and Noah," and instead had Tara's then-little voice saying, "Hello! You've reached Mom, me and my new brother, leave a message at the beep." No, I hadn't murdered the Spawn and buried him in the backyard. He'd dumped me. And I hated telling the tale over and over and over again.

I decided to discuss the biopsy with three people: Michael, of course; Joe—because the funny ha-ha column was not going to be forthcoming; and my crazy friend Ellie, a commitment-phobe worse than Michael, with four broken engagements in the past ten years. She's tried every twelve-step program imaginable and meets an assortment of lovable, if broken men. She always thinks each new guy is "the one." However, despite her questionable taste in men, and a growing collection of diamond rings, she's great company, and Michael and I adore her.

When I got home, Noah was next door with his pal, Jake, and Tara was at track practice. I didn't want them to know anything, so I let Gunther out into the yard and then went upstairs to call Michael, then Ellie. I didn't let on with them, either. I just asked them to meet me for drinks at seven-thirty at The View, this café with a riverfront vista.

Two phone calls down, one to go.

"Joe?"

"*L-A-T-E.* A four-letter word synonymous with your weekly feature."

"Yeah. I have a little problem."

"What? Got stuck in the machine?"

"Very funny."

"I need the column. Either that or you can go for the colonoscopy."

I shuddered.

"No, look…Joe, they spotted something. I have to have a biopsy. The humorous side of squashing my breasts in a machine for your vicarious pleasure just flew out the window."

There was a long pause.

"Hello? Earth to Joe…your *L-A-T-E* writer is *F-R-E-A-K-E-D.*"

"Aw, shit, I can't pick on you for being late if…there's something *really* wrong with you. Other than your terminal tardiness and addiction to shoes. And that attitude of yours."

"Yeah, well, I don't know anything yet, so I'm trying to avoid panic, which isn't easy—even for me. Listen…just keep it under wraps, okay? Run a repeat column, or the one I had scheduled for Sunday. I'll write something new by then."

"All right. And in the meantime, until it turns out to be benign, I'll store up all my complaints so that when you get the good news, I can rip you a new one."

"Appreciate it. Knew I could count on you." I hung

up the phone and smiled. That's when I knew I'd made it as a writer. When Joe started really picking on me. I remember the first time he called me into his office, shut the door and ranted about how I'd offended several of our advertisers by writing about the conspiracy to place women who look like emaciated death camp survivors in their ads. He screamed and yelled about advertisers being our life's blood. Then after his little show for the rest of the staff, who were all eyeballing his office through the glass, he commended me for sticking to my guns. He ran the piece, and the fact that he found my column worth nearly having an aneurysm over told me I was doing all right.

After I hung up with Joe, I stood and faced the mirror over my dresser. I pulled off my shirt and then my bra. My right breast didn't *look* any different from the left. I've always had a love-hate relationship with my breasts and my body—until I passed some magical line of demarcation and began making peace with the fact that so much of what most women obsess over isn't real—it's society's standards for us. My son's sloppy kisses in the morning—they're real. My daughter's moments of fragile adolescent beauty—they're real. Hell, my breasts are real, too, which means that at my age, they're not perched like two unripe hard melons up near my neck somewhere. So they sag a little bit…I'd made peace with them.

I changed into a sweater and some jeans and went downstairs. I made dinner—or what passes for dinner—for Noah and Tara; I'm a member of the 400-Club. Everything in my freezer can be put on a cookie sheet and

cooked at four hundred degrees. God bless chicken nug-
gets. I oversaw homework, and left Noah watching
Nickelodeon and Tara on the phone with Justin. I drove
to The View. Michael and Ellie were waiting.

Michael had a martini—and he'd ordered me one,
too. Ellie had a glass of Zinfandel. Ellie had tried A.A.
once although she's never had a drinking problem.
However, she did meet two lovely recovering alcohol-
ics and got engaged to one. Right now she is in Code-
pendents Anonymous learning how to cure herself of
serial engagements.

I slugged back half my martini. "You know that
mammo I had today?"

"Yeah?" Michael cocked an eyebrow.

"They saw something."

"What?"

"They don't know yet. I have to have a biopsy."

"Oh, shit…" Michael said. "Let's think positive. Do
they think it's—it's—"

"I'm a big girl. You can say it. Cancer? They don't
know."

Ellie patted my hand and then took a tissue out of
her purse.

"Are you *sniveling* already?" I asked her. Ellie had bent
her head full of flaming red curls.

"Yes." She blew her nose.

"Ellie, we don't know a damn thing yet."

"I know, but…I hate medical stuff. My mother had
M.S. Even the sight of the doctor's office makes me
break out in hives."

"You've never had a mammogram?" I knew she was three years older than I was, and in my research prior to my mammogram, I'd discovered women who had children were less at risk than women like Ellie who'd never had and breastfed children.

"No. And you know, I don't think I ever will. I prefer to die oblivious of whatever it is that's going to kill me."

"Ellie… You can't hide your head in the sand."

"Yes, I can."

Michael looked at her. "I'm with you. I hope I die in my sleep."

I stared from Michael to Ellie. "What a supportive friggin' pair you turned out to be. One of you is more chicken than the other. Look, whatever happens, I'm instituting a No Crying rule. I came out with you two to cheer me up. You already have me in a pine box. And for the record, I want to be cremated should something go wrong."

"Nothing's going to go wrong," Michael said soothingly. "Me and you? We've been through too much together. And you're *way* too unpleasant to die. Too bossy. God will keep you down here for a while until you learn your lesson and start learning to work and play well with others."

"Now you're talking…. Will you go with me a week from Friday when I get the biopsy?"

"Wild horses and an evil head nurse with rubber gloves and an enema couldn't keep me away."

"Now you're just being gross."

The three of us ordered another round, and by ten

o'clock, I was sufficiently calmed down enough to go home to bed. Of course the spot was nothing, I told myself. Besides needing to learn to work and play well with others—which I hadn't mastered in kindergarten with the rest of the world—my kids needed me. And so did Michael.

8

Michael

I couldn't sleep. Just the *thought* of Lily needing a biopsy turned my world upside down. And she was right, of course. I am chicken.

Growing up, I did everything to prove I was a redblooded American male. I played every sport, was on every varsity team and screwed every girl who'd let me. But my heart was never into it—women, that is, not sports. I was into baseball so obsessively, I could recite the batting average of every Yankee since the team was formed. I used to spend hours in a batting cage. I'd bat until I had to ice my shoulder when I got home.

I may have been macho on the outside, but inside I was chicken. The thought of admitting I was attracted to men terrified me. But the feeling was there, like a spi-

der on the wall in the corner. Every once in a while, I'd
shine a flashlight beam on that spider. Examine it. Then
I'd turn off the flashlight, too afraid of whatever else was
lurking there.

After I accepted, to myself, that I was gay, I was terrified of being outed.

And after I was finally outed, there was a new fear—
AIDS. And it was Lily who made me shine the flashlight on that fear.

"Come on," she said. She was standing in my apartment, circa 1989—back when I had an ugly black
leather sofa that I used to stick to if I wore shorts when
I sat on it, and LeRoy Neiman prints on my walls—tap-
ping her foot in that impatient way of hers. The big '80s
hair was still big, though not near the heights it was
when I'd first met her. Her pale blue eyes were cold—
she wasn't in the mood for my bullshit.

"Look, Lily, I'm not going. AIDS is a fucking death
sentence, and if I have it, I don't want to know."

I plopped down on my leather couch and averted
my eyes.

"Look, I left Tara with David, and I drove all the way
here. We're going." She came closer to me and stood over
the couch.

"Fuck off, Lily. I'm not going."

When she saw how adamant I was, she sat down on
the coffee table, her knees touching mine, and looked
me in the eyes. "Why? Tell me why, Michael."

My voice cracked. "We've been to four funerals in the

last year. Four. Guys in their prime. Guys who looked like me—healthy, in great shape—who ended up walking cadavers before they ever made it into the casket. I can't remember everyone I've slept with since I was sixteen. Can you?"

She nodded. "Actually, I can. But it doesn't mean I know everyone that they were with. Look…I'm going to be right there to hold your hand, Michael. But you have a moral responsibility to get tested. You could be out there infecting people. And if you're negative, don't you want to know that, too?"

"No. God," I snapped at her and stood up. "Don't you get it? Don't you fucking get it?"

"Get what?"

"You're off playing house with Professor Perfect there. I'm here trying to live my life as a gay man in a straight man's world. And I'm watching men I love—friends, lovers—getting picked off like this is some cosmic game of Russian roulette. There's no cure. There's no hope. So why bother, Lily? I don't want to know."

"Because if you're sick, you could be making other people sick. Sooner or later, the dance has to stop, Michael. You can't be out there screwing around and not caring about the consequences. What about the people who love you?"

"Sure. If I've got AIDS, are you really going to take me—" I inhaled and swallowed hard.

"Take you where?"

"Fuck it. Forget it."

"No. Where?"

"Into your home? Let me sleep on your sheets and eat on your plates? Do you know that when Sammy went home to say goodbye to his family back in Ohio that they made him eat with plastic cutlery? They were afraid to mingle his stuff with theirs in the damn dishwasher. How's that for saying goodbye?"

She looked down at the wedding ring on her hand and then stood up and hugged me. "If you're sick, Michael, yes, I will take you into my home. You can sleep on my sheets and eat on my plates, and you can use my silverware and kiss my baby."

It felt enormous, this thing she'd said, there between us. I started to cry and held onto her. I hadn't been able to cry at a single funeral. I was too worried about whether I had the plague. Too self-involved. I can't have AIDS, I told myself. But I was terrified. Now I cried and let it all out—the fear and the grief.

"Are you getting snot in my hair?"

"Maybe if you didn't tease it so high I wouldn't."

She squeezed me harder. "Come on."

"All right. I'll go. I'll get tested."

We took a cab to a clinic near Christopher Street. The floors were a filthy gray-white, and the place smelled like rubbing alcohol. The plastic chairs in the waiting room were filled with gay men. Some of them already looked sick, and I suppose they were there hoping against hope that the lost weight, the lesions of Karposi's sarcoma wasn't HIV, wasn't AIDS.

The nurse gave me a number. We were identified by number only—the shame and stigma was so great then, not to mention the danger of losing health insurance. I'd have to return in two weeks for my results—they wouldn't give them to you over the telephone for fear you'd blow your brains out or jump out a window if you were positive. Both those options crossed my mind whenever I thought about maybe being positive.

They were the longest two weeks of my life. I couldn't write. I sat at my computer and stared at the screen, the cursor mocking me, taunting me with its blinking. *Queer. Queer. Queer. Sick. Sick. Sick.*

Lily was the one to take me back for my results. During that two-week period, I didn't sleep with anyone. I was too afraid. Too afraid of dying.

We returned to the clinic. More dying men. Lily, of course, was dressed in high heels that clicked along the linoleum when they called my number. She held my hand tightly, both of our palms sweaty. I think I was numb. I barely remember it, as if the whole thing was a dream that happened, almost underwater, like an old Esther Williams's musical.

We were escorted into a private room. "Your test came back negative for HIV." The nurse said it quickly, not prolonging my agony.

I started crying. Lily started crying—actually, she gasped first and then her hand flew to her mouth and she cried silently with relief.

The nurse had compassionate eyes, warm and brown, and absolutely white hair. I guessed she was around sixty. I can't imagine that she had, back in nursing school, pictured one day working in a gay men's clinic.

"It's okay." She patted my hand. "People cry either way."

Lily and I left the clinic and when we got outside to the sidewalk, we grabbed each other and jumped up and down.

"Let's go get drunk," I said. "I feel like celebrating." It was as if someone had just handed me my entire life in a box with a ribbon on it.

9

What I've Learned
by Lily Waters

This last birthday was a Big One. I wish I could get away with saying it was thirty. I told most acquaintances it was thirty-five. But it was actually *that* Big One. I break out in a cold sweat just thinking about it.

What do I have to show for forty years on the planet?

For starters, I have credit card debt so deep I need a shovel to get through the bills each month. A house with a leaky roof. A dog that doesn't come when I call it or sit when I tell it to. (The dog will, however, climb up on the kitchen table to eat out of my son's cereal bowl in the morning.)

I have a closet full of size sixes I no longer fit in, and too many gray hairs to pluck—I'd be bald. I have a hint of crow's-feet, and I spend more on one jar of my anti-wrinkle cream than I used to spend on groceries for an entire month back when I was a struggling reporter.

I have a minivan with nearly 100,000 miles on it, and my kids think I am the least-cool mother on the planet. Me! I was the rebel in high school. I was the girl everyone wanted to hang out with. Now, instead of wearing cute tops, braless, I wear enough underwire to set off the security alarm at the airport.

So would I go back in time and be twenty again?

Not on your life. If I did go back in time, I'd have to give up all this wisdom I've accumulated.

I've learned you really can count your best friends on one hand. They're the ones you can call to nurse you through a broken heart at 2:00 a.m. By forty, you've more than likely held hands with them as you've collectively lost parents or watched a marriage circle the drain, or agonized over children heading down the wrong path, or a boss who seemed determined to make life a living hell. They've seen you with the flu and bad haircuts. You've attended funerals together and weddings. And second weddings. And even a few third weddings. They've learned to love you despite all your flaws because that's what friendship means once you've aged a little bit.

I've learned that growing up means letting go. Suddenly it doesn't seem worth it to carry that grudge against the woman who stole your boyfriend—she can have him! It also means letting go of the dream that somehow your parents will change and undo all the harm and pain they caused you when you were growing up. You must either accept them or feel forever bound and torn apart by the past.

I've learned that no matter how hard I try, I will never be the perfect mother, the perfect friend or the perfect lover. In turn, I've learned to stop demanding perfection from others.

I've learned a lot of other little things, too. Like eating yogurt one day past its expiration date won't kill me, tanning just gives me wrinkles and freckles, and pizza can indeed be a breakfast food when I'm in a rush to get my kids to school on time. I've learned that lipstick is as indispensable as my eyelash curler, and that I really don't need to use conditioner in my hair.

But most of all, I've learned that the reason I'm here is simply to love and be loved in return. All the rest of life…the ups and downs, the checks that bounce and the raise that doesn't cover the cost of living, the messy teen's room and the Magic Marker stain on the carpet, the Kool-Aid spilled on the couch and the bottle of $100-an-ounce perfume your son used to bathe the dog…none of it matters. Not in the face of love.

Sure, love-is-all-you-need sounds like an old Beatles tune. But it really does make life worth living. That's what I've learned. And I wouldn't trade my wisdom for turning back the clock.

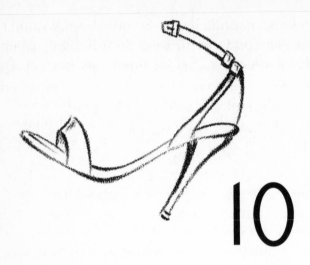

10

Lily

"**Y**ou do realize there's a wire—a *wire*—protruding from my right breast, don't you?" I looked up at Michael and then stared down at this thing—this thin wire, looking like the stuff the orthodontist once threaded through my braces—that was now threaded *into* my breast and sticking out about eight inches.

"Very weird-looking. Does it hurt?"

"Oddly enough, no."

"And the reason for turning your breast into something that would set off the metal detectors at JFK is?"

"It pinpoints the lump exactly and guides the surgeon right to it."

In the time since my mammogram, I'd gone to a breast surgeon who decided to remove the lump instead of just doing a needle biopsy. So now I was waiting for them to come and put me to sleep. When I woke up, I would either have cancer—or not.

"Promise me you won't let them chop my breast off."

"Dr. Costas told you that won't happen."

"Uh-huh. Look, I like him and everything, but I've read plenty of horror stories about doctors taking out the wrong kidney or chopping off the wrong leg."

"Lily, Dr. Costas is one of the best surgeons on the East Coast."

"I know. But maybe he's a closet alcoholic."

"It's eight o'clock in the morning. Even you won't drink a martini this early."

"He could still be drunk from last night."

"Does he seem drunk?"

"No."

A very pretty nurse with short blond hair and a colorful blue and purple smock walked past. Michael caught her eye—easy for him to do since most women are rendered speechless by his good looks. "Excuse me…"

"Yes, sir?"

"Do you have a Valium or something you can give my friend? She's working herself into a frenzy."

"I don't want a Valium," I snapped at him. "I want to wake up with both my breasts!"

The nurse approached my gurney, which was in a little curtained alcove. "Would you like something to calm you down? You'll be going into surgery in about a half hour."

"Well…maybe. A martini?"

She laughed, revealing two deep dimples in her cheeks. She glanced at Michael and then down at me. "Um…no martini, but I can give you something to make you sleepy."

"She'll take it," Michael said insistently.

The nurse disappeared and returned with a syringe. I already had an I.V. She uncapped the needle and inserted it into the I.V. line. Within a minute, I was seeing double.

Michael thanked the nurse and then stroked my forehead. "We've been through a lot together."

"Don't go getting all mushy on me," I whispered sleepily.

"I'm not. I'm stating a fact."

"Yeah. Remember that boyfriend I had who stole my underwear?"

He laughed. "Remember the time I tried to add highlights to my hair? The Duran Duran look?"

"Not pretty. Only a best friend would stand by you after that."

I shut my eyes for a second and felt myself drifting off. Michael's hand on my forehead connected me to reality even as I floated toward dreamland.

"Push!" Michael screamed at me from somewhere in my memories. I glared at him. He had a cool compress on my head and kept trying to stroke my forehead to relax me.

"Stop fucking touching me!"

"Push, Lily."

It had been seven years since I gave birth to Tara, and now Noah was being born in the middle of a snowstorm while my poor husband, David, was stranded in Manhattan, with no trains operating out to the 'burbs.

"Come on, Lily," Michael pleaded with me. "Push!"

"How many fucking kids have *you* pushed out?" The pain was searing, starting in my back, and I felt like I was literally splitting in two.

"Breathe!"

The doctor between my legs said, "Concentrate, Lily."

I glared at her, too. "I can't." Suddenly, this wave of exhaustion took over the pain, and I collapsed back against the pillows. I could hear the baby's heartbeat on the monitor and a steady *beep-beep* of machines. I had my relaxation tape on. Fuck Lamaze. I mean, I love a little Wyndham Hill and jazz as much as the next person, but piano music and a pan flute aren't going to transport me to my fucking happy place.

Dr. Gorman looked at Michael. "She needs to push with each contraction now. The baby's head is right here. I see a head of black hair."

Michael leaned up close to me, his voice in my ear. "You can do this, Lily. You've done everything you've ever put your mind to, gotten every job you wanted, every assignment. You can get this baby out of you. Find your inner bitch and push."

"Get—the—fuck—away—from—me!" I grunted as another contraction came. They were in waves now overtaking me time and again until I felt like I was drowning in pain. But his pep talk made me lean up on my elbows a bit and push.

"Atta girl!"

"Don't 'atta girl' me!"

Another contraction. Michael pulled on my left thigh and a nurse on my right.

"I'm not a wishbone," I shrieked.

"Quiet, Lily," Dr. Gorman snapped. "Concentrate."

So I did. I thought of how desperately I wanted to hold this baby. I was tired of practically needing a fork-lift to climb out of bed. Tired of not being able to see my feet or tie my sneakers. I wanted a baby to snuggle.

"A few more pushes," Dr. Gorman said excitedly.

"Come on, Lily," Michael urged.

And then with a burst of energy from Lord knows where—maybe the thought of getting to have my favorite martinis again and fit into my old jeans—the baby's head popped out, then a shoulder and…Dr. Gorman plopped him on my chest.

"It's a boy!"

I started crying. Michael started crying. I counted ten fingers. I counted ten toes. He was covered in sticky whiteness and had blood on his face, but he was here. My angel, Noah.

Michael stroked my forehead. "I knew you could do it."

"I guess I did, too. What was I supposed to do, leave him halfway in and halfway out?" I laughed.

He kissed my forehead. "You made a life."

Michael cut the cord, and the baby was taken to the nursery. I was exhausted. The doctor gave me a shot of Demerol for the pain—I'd had a pretty major episiotomy. In a few minutes, drowsiness took over. Michael stroked my forehead and pushed my hair, which was matted to my cheeks from the sweat and pushing of labor, off my face. I felt his fingers, connecting me to reality, even as I floated away to dream of Noah.

After I came to, maybe three hours later, my surgeon appeared looking grim-faced. Apparently, he hadn't liked what he'd sliced from my breast. I wanted to accuse him of being drunk on the job, but I didn't. I just shut my eyes when he was done talking to me and pretended I was still out of it from the anesthesia. I didn't want to talk to Michael. I didn't want to talk to Ellie, who had taken a half day from her job as a graphic artist and come to the hospital to sit with Michael and wait. I didn't want to talk to anyone. So I shut my eyes and tried to go someplace serene.

Despite what the radiologist at the women's center said, she was full of shit. Three weeks later, I could safely say it *wasn't* the not knowing that was the worst of it. It was the knowing. I had cancer. Suddenly I had an oncologist named Dr. Morris. And my column was completely wrecked. I went from writing about kneading dough in a mammogram to writing about mortality.

I still tried to be funny. With the doctors and nurses. With the guy who had come to suck the last pint of blood I had out of my arm for tests and more tests. With the insurance company even. I made them all laugh to show them that I wasn't afraid.

But, of course, I was.

They just didn't have to know that.

No one did.

A week or so after my surgery I had to go for an on-cology consult. Dr. Morris wanted to discuss the lymph node biopsies, the whole thing. I knew I had cancer. Just not how bad. But Dr. Morris told me. I knew it wasn't good, just from the way his large mitt of a hand enveloped mine. I noticed his gold wedding band was scratched and worn. I noticed the hair on his hands was pale blond mixed with gray. His watch was a Bulova, and it had the date in a little square where the three should have been and a burgundy alligator-skin wristband. I observed all this as he patted the top of my hand and then settled his to rest on mine. Dr. Morris seemed like the kind of guy who only holds hands when he has bad news. It was a dead giveaway.

"Look, Doc, we must stop meeting this way." A clock on his bookshelf went *tick, tick, tick* in the silence as he looked at me.

"Lily…" his blue-gray eyes watered just enough for me to notice. Then he cleared his throat. "It's an aggressive cancer."

My breath still left me, and I had to remind myself to inhale. Breathe, Lily, breathe. I felt like I had a case of the bed spins, my world twirling around me, confirming what I sensed. What I'd dreamed about at night since the surgery. Monsters and serial killers chasing me. Just like the cancer. Finding me no matter where I hid. I think I knew it even as they were scanning my body, and the faint hum of hospital machinery whispered around me, but I still blinked and stared at him. I still stopped breathing.

"Fuck." I exhaled unevenly. "What the hell am I going to tell my kids?" I heard the catch of self-pity in my voice and looked out the window at the expanse of parking lot behind the hospital.

"You've made every one of my nurses laugh today. You've made Dr. Costas laugh. He told me how special you are.... You've got to keep a positive attitude."

"Easy for you to say, Doc. You don't have the Big C. And no offense, but you have no hair—and I am rather fond of mine and it's all going to go bye-bye."

He patted the top of his head. "Bald can be beautiful."

"Look at me. Do I look like the kind of woman who has cancer? I look perfectly healthy. I feel like…like I'm sleepwalking." I paused. I had been telling myself that it would be all right. That it would be "good cancer"— whatever that is—less aggressive.

"This really…is inconvenient."

He gave me a half smile. "I don't guess there's ever a convenient time to get cancer."

"Well, I'll look in my calendar and pencil it in when I'm really old and decrepit. This just—God, it sucks."

"I wrestle with that in this job every day. People ask me how I can deal with cancer day in and day out. But honestly, it's patients like you that make it bearable. You have a fighter's attitude. But I don't pretend to understand God's plan."

"How bad is it? How aggressive?"

"It's in your lymph nodes. We have to schedule a body scan to see if it's spread anywhere else. The lumpectomy got the cancer—but the edges weren't well-de-

fined. We biopsied lymph nodes under your arm-
pit…um…it's pretty bad. I have this report and we're
going to go over all of it. I don't like my patients kept
in the dark. I'd rather you know what you're looking at
so you can fight."

"So we're gearing up for a battle?"

"No. I won't lie to you. It's a war. But I'm up for it if
you are."

"This really means bye-bye hair."

He nodded.

"I could go for a platinum wig. Or hot pink."

"Hot pink would be flattering."

"Am I going to die?"

"No predictions. I don't believe in breaking things
down into statistics. Wouldn't you rather be the one who
defies the statistics?"

"Sure. But the losing-hair thing sucks."

"You don't have to shave your legs then. Have to look
at the bright side."

"When I'm boyfriendless I never shave them much
anyway. But I see where you're going with that."

We talked some more, talked about chemo and radiation. But mostly it was more hand-holding. More con-
soling. More jokes.

I left his office and went and sat in my van and tried
to cry. The c-word. Aggressive.

But I was too stunned to cry.

When I got to my sleepy little town up the Hudson
River from Manhattan, I smelled a first snow—super
early that year—in the air and found my senses alive in

ways only those who are sick can understand. I drove home from the train station and stood in front of my Cape Cod house, shingled in white with royal blue shutters, looking at the huge jack-'o-lantern with a candle inside reflecting an orange glow out onto the street.

Michael, of course, was in the kitchen when I walked in, cooking. He's the reason Tara and Noah eat anything of nutritional value. I had tried to cook scrambled eggs for Noah the day before and had burned them terribly. They were brown and yellow with this sort of brown-black skin clinging to the top of them. Noah had looked at me with his baleful brown eyes and asked, "What's wrong with my eggs, Mom?"

"They're suntanned. Eat them. Trust me, they're better that way." He was not convinced.

I pulled off my boots, silently thanking God for Michael. The sounds of opera echoed through the house. Michael was playing a Boccelli CD as he prepared, from the looks of the pans when I went in the kitchen, enough food to feed all the citizens of New York City and still have doggie bags left over. But that's Michael. Always big, big, big. He cooks the way his heart is, generous and full. He wants to stuff you with his love. The fact that he never gains an ounce totally makes me despise him, but he is my best friend, so I allow him this one small failing.

"What's for supper?" I asked, taking off my black peacoat and my new favorite scarf, an Hermés that Michael had bought me. He had been beyond supportive since the surgery, and I think the scarf was in anticipation for what was next. Music filled the kitchen. Boccelli's a man Michael and I both agree on.

"Mom!" Noah's face lit up as I entered my least favorite room in the house. "Uncle Michael's teaching me to make…what is it again?"

"Pâte brisée, for starters, and linguine with white clam sauce à la Angelo."

"Sounds heavenly," I murmured. "Where's Tara?"

"Where else?" Noah said, sitting on the counter so he could see what Michael was simmering in the saucepan.

"Justin's?"

Noah rolled his eyes as he did every time Tara swooned over a phone call from her new—actually, first—boyfriend. "Mom's a genius," Noah giggled.

"And don't you forget it, Champ." I smiled, pinching his cheek.

Michael looked over his shoulder at me, and of course, without my saying a word, he read it on my face.

"Noah, honey," Michael said, "we're just going to let this absorb some of the garlic flavor. Why don't you go play on your computer, and I'll call you when it's time to set the table."

"Okay."

Michael lifted my little boy, with his lopsided grin and missing two front teeth, down from the counter, and sent him off to his room with a kiss on the top of his head.

"Well?" Michael turned to me, his black eyes filled with worry.

"It's not good, Michael. It was in the lymph nodes."

"You're too young. How is this possible?"

"It just is, Michael," I snapped. "So though I know you had high hopes for setting me up with your sexy stud of an accountant, I would say unless he digs bald chicks, all bets are off."

"Don't even talk like that, Lily. I hate when you do that."

"I *can* talk like that. I'm the one with cancer."

"Lily…"

I saw him swallow hard and look away. "The rule, Michael!"

"Oh, fuck your No Crying rule. Who institutes something as stupid as that? Just fuck it, Lily. I'm allowed to cry." He exhaled loudly and turned his head. In profile, he was even more good-looking, which I have come to believe over the nearly twenty years I've known him should be against all laws of genetics. His nose was perfectly straight and regal. There was strength and beauty in his cheekbones and jawline, in his olive complexion and black curly hair. His neck was strong, like a Greek marble bust.

He faced me again. "Sorry. I was having a moment. God, Lily," he wrapped his arms around me, and I leaned my head against his chest. I fit so perfectly, as if the hollow there was made for me. More often than not, I suppose I shared that hollow with his latest lover, but they always left and I was always here. For now. I snuggled in closer. His black sweater smelled of Aramis.

"Hello chemo. Goodbye hair."

I heard him sniffling.

"Are you blowing your nose in my ear?"

"You need some new one-liners. Honestly, you can

be…the most impossible bitch. It's a good thing I adore you."

"I'm the only one who can put up with you during Yankees season. And now you've corrupted my son."

"Taken him to the dark side."

"Baseball is so boring."

"Blasphemer!" He pulled back in mock horror.

I smiled. "I love you, Michael."

"I love you, Lily."

"Now we really have to tell the kids. I don't think I can hide a bald head, and you know I am the biggest baby in the world about throwing up."

"I'm well aware…. Are you going to tell Satan's Spawn?"

"No."

"One of the kids might tell him."

"He hasn't called either of them in going on five months."

"Such an asshole. All right then. And by the way, just because you have cancer doesn't mean you get out of clean-up duty."

"I wouldn't mind, but do you have to use every pan in the kitchen? Every one?"

"You won't be complaining when you taste." He held a spoon of clam sauce to my mouth.

"You are a culinary genius."

"More flattery. It'll get you everything."

"A cure? Can I have that?" I smiled weakly.

"I'll talk to the Big Man and see what I can do."

Michael attended Mass every Sunday, a fact that confused me. Some of his dates found it endearing. I didn't understand how he could be a gay Catholic, technically condemned by the very Church whose faith sustained him. I just didn't understand, though being sick had taught me in a short amount of time to stop questioning faith. Mine was fragile. My faith. Barely there, it was like the last breaths of a dying person, just a whisper of air, a hint of life. With Michael, faith was like greedily gulping in the wind at the seaside, filling his lungs with its healing.

We sat down for dinner, just the three of us. Michael said grace. "Heavenly Father, grant us a miracle. In the name of Jesus Christ, Amen."

"What kind of miracle do you want?" Noah asked with simple innocence.

Michael looked at me. I shook my head.

"We're praying your mother doesn't burn your breakfast tomorrow. But that may be too much to ask."

Noah nodded, looking at me the way little boys do when they adore their mothers.

I stared up at the ceiling and said my own silent prayer. *Big Man, breakfast I can handle. A battle with cancer, I'm not so sure.*

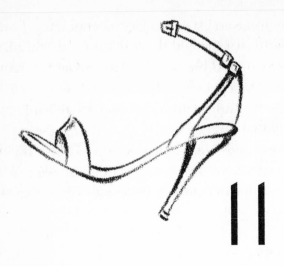

11

Michael

I've been single since the 1980s. Since the age of AIDS.

Lily and I used to attend funerals like they were dates. It seemed, for a time, that we had one funeral a week. It's so hard to convey to anyone not living in Manhattan or San Francisco or Los Angeles at that time what it was like. Lily worked for a newspaper and freelanced at magazines. I wrote for some magazines and taught. We were around some of New York's best creative people—graphic designers and writers, playwrights and poets. We were in our twenties and believed we were invincible, that we were having the time of our lives. Only for some of us, it was borrowed time.

One by one, people started dropping. Friends who were beautiful young men not a month before when we

saw them had Karposi's, their faces covered with the pur-
plish lesions that marked them the way leprosy used to
mark its victims. They grew sicker and sicker, some of
them going insane before the end, often alone, just skel-
etons, disowned by family, ignored by neighbors—or
worse, vilified.

A lover of mine, one I buried in 1987, once asked me
when I knew I was gay. It was a rare moment when we
weren't fighting or drunk or breaking each other's hearts
with our cheating and lies. We were lying in my king-
size bed, staring at the ceiling after smoking a joint, and
he asked me, "When did you know?"

I shrugged.

"Come on, Michael. You always shut me out every
time I try to get to know you."

"I didn't shut you out ten minutes ago." I grinned,
then, as always, aware that my looks offered me a sanc-
tuary. A grin. A seduction. Hiding always came so easily to me.

"Come on. When did you know?"

I thought about it in my pot-fogged mind. "Part of
me wants to say I always knew. I was born knowing. But
I guess it was in junior high when everyone was paying
dollars—whole dollars!—to look at a magazine of
Swedish porno that my friend Greg's father brought
back from one of his trips overseas. Mr. Morgan was a
pilot. It was hardcore stuff, and Greg found it in the bottom of his father's sock drawer. Blond women with
enormous tits screwing two guys at once, a lot of times
black men. Some kind of Swedish obsession. All my

buddies were going ga-ga over the blonde, and I was going crazy over these pictures of cocks the size of loaves of French bread."

"That was a good clue," he laughed. And then, like the two high idiots we were, we laughed ourselves silly for fifteen minutes until we couldn't even remember what we were laughing at anymore.

He was dead eleven months later. Not that it stopped me. I never thought anything would stop me. Not the AIDS crisis. Not my own HIV scare—I'm negative, though, thank God. Not lovers settling down into couplehood. I eventually got tested, but I was still running from myself. And then Noah was born.

Noah Michael Waters (middle name after yours truly) was born at five o'clock in the morning the night of a massive blizzard. Lily's ex, David, who was not yet an ex, was stranded in a Manhattan snowstorm (and please, what bullshit that turned out to be) with no trains leaving the city. I had gone to keep Lily company before the storm hit and ended up sleeping on Lily's couch. If the new baby decided to make a grand entrance, I didn't want to worry that I couldn't get to her.

Just before midnight, Lily came downstairs and poked me.

"Michael?" she whispered. "My water broke."

The next fifteen minutes played like an *I Love Lucy* episode. I panicked. I jumped off the couch and started putting on my Reeboks with no socks—which was fucking frigid in the snow. I was running around look-

ing for my coat, looking for Lily's coat, running into the
bathroom to brush my teeth, screaming, "Be calm, Lily.
Be calm!"

Lily just laughed. "We have a little time yet, Michael.
But with the snow we better get going." She called up
her next-door neighbor, a sweet older lady named Marjorie, to come and stay with Tara.

"Breathe…breathe…" I urged Lily. "You can do this
naturally."

"Fuck that. I want my epidural as soon as we get
there."

I kept watching Lily, expecting the baby to drop down
between her legs at any moment.

"Michael, I am not going to be seen with you dripping toothpaste down your chin. Go wash. I'll wait."

Marjorie arrived, her hair in plastic rollers held in
place with bobby pins, and a thick bathrobe on. She
hugged Lily for good luck. Before we left, we went upstairs to kiss Tara goodbye. She was eight and cute then,
not the petulant teen she is now. "Bring me home a sister," she murmured sleepily. I warmed up Lily's "mom
van," which I had mercilessly teased her about when she
got it. She'd sold out, gone suburban on me. She moved
out of the city when she married Spawn, only then we
didn't call him that.

I drove slowly, trying to see through the swirls of
snow dancing in my headlights. Next to me, Lily kept
breathing. I was a pinch hitter. I hadn't gone through
Lamaze. I just knew, when David got stranded in the
city, that I might be "it," and she had given me a crash

course in the fact that she would soon be screaming, hitting me and otherwise behaving in decidedly insane fashion while she, in turn, tried to push this baby out of her.

"Breathe," I said, my eyes squinting in the poor visibility.

"I am," she shouted back and slugged me in the arm.

"I mean *me*. I'm talking to myself. You're making me nervous."

"Fuck you, Michael. Just get me to the hospital. *I want my epidural!*"

We pulled into the parking lot of St. Mary's hospital, and I got her a wheelchair and pushed her up to maternity. Everyone assumed I was the father, and she and I laughed each time the mistake was made. At the same time, she didn't call David to tell him she'd gone into labor. I think she knew…maybe she was afraid at that perfect moment, delivering this new baby, that another woman would answer the phone in his hotel room and ruin it for her.

I held her hand. I breathed with her. I watched the baby's heartbeat on the monitor. I gave her ice chips, even as she screamed at me.

"I don't want fucking ice chips! I want a ginger ale. A Coke. A frigging martini. Something. Please. Just a sip."

I gave the nurse a pleading look, but she shook her head and spoke as one soothes a child.

"Now Lily, you've had one child already. You know you can't have anything to drink. Just ice chips."

As soon as the nurse left to check on another patient,

Lily's lips quivered, and she whimpered, "Michael, just one sip. Go find a soda. I just want one sip."

"I can't, Lily, honey. You heard her."

"What the fuck does she know?" she screamed and punched me in the arm again. I decided giving birth was like having multiple personalities.

Hours later, in a mirror the nurses set up for us, I watched Noah's head crown. I was amazed at how a woman's body could *do* that. Stretch to let this new life emerge, covered in blood and white stuff Lily assured me was normal. He was whole and perfect.

When he cried, I cried. Lily cried. I cut the cord, terrified and amazed at separating this new life from his mother with a snip. The doctor placed him on his mother's breast, and Noah immediately searched for her nipple, found it, and started making sucking noises. I put my finger next to his little fist, and he grabbed it. I counted five little perfect fingers. Then he stopped sucking, turned his face and stared at me as I said, "Hello, Noah." I convinced myself he knew my voice from all the talks Lily and I had during her pregnancy about how David was growing distant. She was certain he was having an affair. And I had been there for her, listening and talking. My voice.

Lily sniffled and laughed and cried at the same time. "He knows you, Michael."

They took Noah from us and put him on a scale to weigh him and do tests and clean him up. And I was aware that everything had changed. I had witnessed this life, and I felt responsible for the little guy. I was there when he took his first breath. I was part of something…someone who was now going to grow up and become a person. A man who might become president or, better yet, a starter for the Yankees. And I wanted to be part of creating that.

Ordinarily, I would have gone home that night, changed and cruised the bars. I had safe sex since finding out I was HIV negative, but though I had sworn to change my ways, I hadn't. I mean, yeah, I wore a condom, but I still didn't allow myself to stand still for very long. I was always running. Running from what? The past, I guess. Everyone but Lily, who knew so much about me that running from her would have been futile.

But instead of going back to my apartment, after Noah was born, I slept on the couch in Lily's birthing room, and while she slept, I held him and whispered, "Whatever happens between your mom and dad, Noah Michael, I will be here for you. I'll never abandon you. I'll never judge you. Whoever you become, whoever you are in that soul of yours, I'll accept. I may have a problem if you don't like baseball, but we can work around that."

David left Lily six weeks later, for good. No looking back. She had gone to the grocery store and by the time she made it back home, his bags were packed. The fact that I had been an usher in their wedding made me not want to believe what she had been telling me throughout the pregnancy. I told her what *I* wanted to hear— what I thought *she* wanted to hear—not the truth, which was that any guy who had as many excuses for not making it home from the city as he did was surely fucking someone on the couch in his office.

Lily was a mess. If it hadn't been for me and the kids—especially this new little infant all baby-smelling (they really do smell perfect)—I think she would have curled up and quit. But Lily is a fighter. Lord *knows* she is a fighter.

His girlfriend-on-the-side, the Child Bride as we call her, was an exchange student from London, and he moved there to marry her as soon as the divorce was final. Noah, in some ways, was mine. David never looked to the past, and I never wanted him to. Lily was better off without him. And instead of Noah's real father, it was me who witnessed all the miracles. The first tooth, the first step, the first day of school. And wrapped up in this package of childhood was a gift. A gift of my own mortality.

Where some men might see their son and think they are immortal, for they are now passing on their genes, I saw so clearly how I would one day die. Noah was the future, and from the moment he grasped my pinky in his little fist, I wanted to pass along all my knowledge of the batting averages for the entire Yankees lineup since 1972, the secrets of a perfect soufflé, the stance when you're at bat, my record collection that I refused to part with—including The Village People and Etta James and Beverly Sills. I wanted him to learn it was okay for a boy to like opera and baseball. I wanted to read *David Copperfield* aloud to him. I wanted to take him to the Metropolitan and show him Chagall and Degas, and my favorite, Goya. I wanted to save him from Lily's deadly cooking. I wanted to live on, through Noah.

After all the death I had seen. All the funerals, all the bed sores and Karposi's scabs. All the dementia and pneumonia that was so much a part of the AIDS crisis before the cocktails that keep them all alive now, I was ready for a gift of life. So Noah was a gift of my mortality, of seeing I would some day be gone and knowing I wanted to leave my mark, and also a gift of life and innocence in an age lacking those very things. He was my boy then and now. He changed me forever.

I thought Lily and I had shared the toughest stuff there was. The good stuff, too. We had danced on tabletops in the Palladium, and we had taken a cruise together to the Bahamas. And we had survived her marriage. I mean, for a lot of friends, marriage is the death knell. They drift apart. But we didn't. Secretly, I think David always had one foot in, one foot out; he never committed with his whole heart to her. So I was convenient. I got to absorb some of her intensity, her passion, her excitement. He got to remain a little distant.

Divorce always sucks—but I can't imagine being postpartum hormonal and facing it. But we got through that. We got through my attending my grandmother's funeral—my father hasn't spoken to me since I came out in college. But cancer? I mean, cancer is always something that happens to someone *else's* family. Oh, you know, this guy I work with, his sister's brother-in-law has a brain tumor. It's never up close and personal. Only now it wasn't someone else. It was Lily.

12

Curveball
An excerpt from a novel by Michael Angelo

Sam opened his locker and a giant black dildo fell out. Not that he'd seen too many dildos, but this one was enormous, and it was wrinkled and life-like. A giant black cock.

When the dildo fell, Sam felt eyes boring into him from behind. He didn't turn around. He didn't acknowledge the thing. A burning filled his eyes, tears he willed away. *This is just locker room horseshit. I will not let them see me cry. I won't.*

But the tears were there. Sam had never felt so alone his entire life. Charlie, who had been a constant since the first day of orientation freshman year, had stopped speaking to him. Charlie slept at his girlfriend's dorm room every night and wouldn't look at Sam in class. Let alone the locker room.

And now, the dildo.

He could hear them snickering. But not a good kind of laughter. He heard the menace in it. Worse, he could feel a heat in the room. They may have been laughing, but they hated him. Like a flash of lightning striking the ground, an electric current seemed to pass from one guy to the other, and Sam could feel the heat growing.

He kept his back to them, but then he was aware two of them, his teammates—guys he'd spent three years with, on buses going to away games, getting drunk with, celebrating wins in the fall, and working harder in the hot days of spring following losses—were now next to him. Too close. In his space.

He could see them, sense them seething, from the corner of his eye. And then he was punched in the side of the head.

Sam had been in fights before. In seventh grade, he was jumped on the playground. But in high school, he had grown taller, developed his muscles, become a big-man-on-campus jock, and no one fucked with him. He was tough, but he wasn't a fighter. He guessed his team was going to make him one.

He reeled from the shot to his head, crashed into his own locker, and then wheeled around, raising his fists and swinging, hoping to fight his way out of the locker room.

But there were ten of them and one of him. They kicked him and he remembered being pelted, full force, by baseballs hurled, he knew, by one of the pitchers who had a fast ball clocked at ninety miles per hour.

They were also hurling names at him. *Queer. Faggot. Homo.* Then he felt a bat land on his ribs and he heard a crack.

"No, no…" Charlie's voice rose above the cacophony. "Off of him!"

The locker room was a total mess by now. Guys started pulling each other off of Sam. He was barely conscious, aware that he was slumped, unable to stand fully upright, blood pouring from his mouth. He could feel he'd lost a tooth. His nose was broken. He couldn't breathe without pain. But mercifully, Charlie was going to stop this. So Sam had fallen in love with him, but they still were best friends. Had been best friends. That would win out over this insanity.

"Hand me the bat," Charlie commanded to the one who'd struck him. "The bat is *mine.*" And with that, Charlie swung, as hard as Sam had ever seen him swing, and hit Sam, twice, in the gut. He didn't know what was worse, knowing they were going to kill him, or knowing Charlie was capable of it.

Sam fell to the floor, his head against the cool locker room tile. Charlie tossed the bat on the ground, and the team filed out, leaving Sam there. They shut off the lights. He couldn't even get to a phone to call an ambulance for himself.

Sam blacked out. His last thought was of Charlie. All he had done was fall in love with him.

13

Lily

Justin is Tara's first love, and she is over-the-moon crazy about him. She comes home from their dates and tells me all the details—what he said, what he wore, that he held her hand or kissed her good-night. Tara and I have always been close, but now that she is fifteen, I am also subjected to her withering glares and her mercurial displays of temper. I was certain she would feel my getting cancer was a giant inconvenience to her social schedule.

Michael said he would tell Noah. I just felt emotionally beat-up, and agreed. But I had to tell Tara.

She didn't hear my knock on her bedroom door the first three times, so I poked my head in. The music was deafening, but I smiled as I suffered through it. At least

I could make out the lyrics, and thank God she doesn't like rap. Whatever happened to Debbie Harry and Blondie? To the Rolling Stones? I know what happened to the Stones. They got wrinkled. Poster boys for what drugs, alcohol and groupies can do to your youthful complexion. For the thousandth time, I thanked my late mother for insisting on sunscreen when all my friends were slathering on baby oil and sunning themselves. I had the least-cool mom (heredity?) in the neighborhood—and now I had been the least wrinkled woman at my high school reunion two years ago. Except for Carol Lundt, who'd already "had work" done. She'd had so much Botox injected she looked like her face was frozen.

"Tara, honey?" I cooed, poking my head in her door. Her long brown hair was pulled up in a ponytail, and her green eyes had just the slightest hint of mascara on the lashes. She has a runner's build, thin and muscular. She ran the 100-meter and 200-meter for her high school this year.

"Mom! Have you heard of *knocking?*" she shouted as she sat on her bed doing her nails.

"Tara, have you heard of *headphones?*" I shouted back. She rolled her eyes and turned down the music.

"How's Justin?"

"Perfect," she grinned, and put the top back on her nail polish. She wears blue, which I find hideous, but as a mother of a teenager, I have learned to choose my battles. Blue nail polish, belly shirts, the occasional experimentation with pink streaks in her hair, the four piercings in her ears—but not in her belly button, thank God—the messy room…these I back off on. I even stopped caring when she opts for a Diet Coke and a Pop-Tarts pastry for breakfast. But drugs…alcohol…she knows where I draw the line.

"Sometimes I wish I was your age and falling in love for the first time." I felt myself well up. If I was fifteen, then I wouldn't be forty with cancer.

"Tara—" my heart felt like it was going to burst out of my chest "—I have to tell you something."

"What?" She waved her hands in the air to dry her nails.

"You know how I had to have that mammogram from my column and then get that cyst removed?" I sat down on her bed. It had a comforter that was the most hideous shade of deep purple with pink beading on it. "Choose your battles" was my constant mantra. The comforter matched the grape-colored walls.

"Yes…" she said slowly, warily. Maybe she was willing me not to tell her, because I am sure in that instant she knew what was going to follow as surely as I knew when Dr. Morris put his hand on mine.

"I have cancer."

She looked away from me. I longed to take her hand, but I knew in her teenage way she would have just yelled at me for smudging her nail polish.

"Shit!"

"Don't say shit."

"I can say shit, Mom. My mother has *cancer*."

Choosing my battle, I just nodded. In the grand scheme of things, what's a "shit" when you've got cancer? Fuck, I should let her get the tattoo and belly piercing with that reasoning.

She rolled her eyes, which were filling with tears. "How bad? I mean…are you going to die? Is it that bad?"

"I don't think I'm going to die, no. I don't plan on it. But I can't promise. I mean, I could walk outside tomorrow and get hit by a bus."

"Sure. Like this is a high-speed bus zone, Mom."

"Anyone ever tell you that you're very sarcastic?"

"I wonder where I get it from?" she snapped. Then I heard her inhale deeply a few times. "I can't believe this! It's not fair. It's not fair, Mom. Everything seemed to be going fine. Great. Track team this year, Justin, getting to go to Homecoming. Why do you have to have cancer? Why? What did this family do wrong? Huh? First, my father leaves us and doesn't even bother to write or call us. He's the world's biggest dick…and now my mother gets cancer."

It was like a verbal slap, but I knew she was just venting what I felt. I could accept that life wasn't fair. I mean, I'd been accepting it since I was Tara's age. My mother refused to buy me Jordache jeans and insisted I wear Sears. Might as well hang a Social Reject sign on your kid. I told my mom it wasn't fair and got the first of thousands of "Life isn't fair, Lilianna Elizabeth." Of course, I had rebelled against her and spent every spare dollar I got babysitting on cool clothes. But I didn't imagine there were enough babysitting dollars in the world to level the playing field when it came to cancer.

"I wish I had an answer, Tara. But if I go down that

path, down the not-fair path, I'll never get off of it. Life isn't fair." Christ, my mother emerged from my mouth again.

"Please. Uncle Michael tells me that all the time."

"You should listen to him for a change." I smiled.

"Look, the rosary bead routine is fine for Noah, but I have a lot of questions for the Big Man Upstairs. Like why *my* mother? Why you? When everything seemed to be going so perfect?"

With that, Tara dissolved into tears and flung herself at me, smudging her nails and not caring, crying and clinging to me. I held onto her, enjoying having her in my arms for this moment, smelling her hair, and feeling a surge of mother-love that only other mothers can understand. Michael has taught me so much about music, and I think of it as a crescendo, this mountainous rise and swell until you feel as if your heart will burst. It reminds me of the chorus in Beethoven's Ninth. That she needed me because I had told her I was sick made the moment bittersweet, but I would take it. The hug, the holding. For the moment, she was my baby again.

After a minute or two, she pulled away and wiped her eyes. "Damn, my nails. Figures. Nothing is going right. Shit." She glared at me as if willing me to pick a fight over the word.

"Do you want to talk about it?"

"What?"

"The cancer."

"No. I *hate* that word. I don't want to talk about it. I want to call Justin and pretend I am an ordinary kid, not some girl whose life is like a movie of the week, you know?"

I stood up and kissed her cheek. "I love you."

"Love you, too."

I turned and stepped over the piles of laundry on the floor, and walked out of her cluttered bedroom and down the hall into my own. I had installed a private phone line in Tara's room six months before or I'd never be able to talk on the phone in my own house.

I called up Michael, who had moved to the 'burbs himself two years ago, and had Noah for the night.

"Hello?"

"Hey Michael, how's Noah?"

"Sleeping. God I love them when they're asleep. They're a lot less work then, you know?"

"You're preaching to the choir, gay choirboy."

"You know I don't wear anything under my choir robes, right?"

"Yet another visual I don't need…. So did you tell him yet?"

"Yeah. He cried, but you know, I think he took it pretty well. He asked if Mom was going to die and all that. I told him, 'Noah we all die someday.'"

"You know, one of these days we're both going to have to come up with some new lines."

"I know. My credibility is lagging."

I grew silent.

"What?" he asked.

"Nothing. I was just thinking I wish we didn't have to spout lines like 'whoever said life was fair' and all that."

"Yes. I would like to not have to come up with all the answers. It's difficult being brilliant, you realize."

"And so modest."

"Certainly. And so fucking good-looking."

"Thanks for telling him. He idolizes you, though Lord knows you don't need anyone else worshipping you. Is that woman from the gym still calling you?"

"Yes. Seems like ever since she found out I was gay, she's determined to bed me and change me. Why can't she think 'what a waste of gorgeous manhood' like the rest of them?"

"You are impossible. Anyway, thanks for telling him. I just...I feel like I'm on my last raw nerve right now. And thanks for keeping him overnight."

"Anytime, Lily. Has Spawn called by any chance?"

"No. I got a card today. He sent me an extra hundred dollars in his child support check and told me to buy them each something they wanted for their birthdays."

"Does he realize he missed Tara's by three months?"

"I'm sure Child Bride didn't want him sending anything extra at all. Have I told you lately how much I hate them?"

"It's their loss, Lily."

"I know. Funny thing is the kids just don't seem to care anymore."

"Well, they have you."

"For now."

"Stop talking like that. You're going to beat it."

"I can't even picture losing my hair. I'll never complain about a bad hair day again."

"We'll take it day by day."

"Oh…I meant to tell you thanks for the flowers today. They were a great pick-me-up. You're perfect in every way but one, darling."

"I know. You'd marry me in a heartbeat if I wasn't gay."

"No. I was thinking about your obsession with the Yankees. It's a sickness."

"You know, I just cannot stand it when you emotionally batter me this way. Next thing you know you're going to tell me Don Mattingly shouldn't be on the greatest team ever."

Michael has this little game he plays for every sport. He compiles a list of the "greatest team ever"—thus Mattingly could play with Babe Ruth, Lou Gehrig and Mickey Mantle, despite the fact that they were not contemporaries.

"He can be on your greatest team ever, but I find your whole greatest-team-ever thing a tad high schoolish."

"Well, you know my emotional maturity level…."

"Yes, I do. My very own Peter Pan."

"I better get going, Lil. I need to finish grading these horrible term papers. What are they *teaching* them in high school? Certainly not how to write in complete sentences."

"'Night, Michael."

"Love you."

"Love you, too."

I hung up the telephone. Now my secret was less of a secret. Tara and Noah knew…and little by little, I'd have to tell other people. My parents were no longer living—and I was an only child—so my friends were my family. Crabby Joe was my family. I had to tell other people soon, though. I felt my hair. My soon-to-be-bald head was going to be like an announcement to the world. I have the c-word.

14

Michael

Lily is not a pretty picture when she is throwing up. I suppose no one is, but she is especially hideous, and I know she won't mind me saying so.

I held a pot under her head and pulled back her hair because she couldn't make it into the bathroom. Vomit came out her nose. So much for the antiemetics.

"I can't do this," she moaned. "I cannot do another six months of this. It's fucking hell."

"I can tell you holding this pot isn't thrilling me either, Sugarcakes."

"Fuck you."

In truth, I wanted her mad at me. Angry people don't give up. Depressed people, pessimistic people, the people who always see the damn glass as half-empty—they give up. Angry people fight. They do not go quietly into this good night.

"After all we've been through," I said. "We come to this. Me holding your barf bag."

I heard her laugh, though her face was bent away from me and I couldn't see her smile. Laughing was good. Laughing people get well. I'd read Norman Cousins's book. Laughter really was a kind of medicine. So we had laughter and anger—I was covering both the bases.

"So," I said casually, "did I tell you that I invited Joe over for wine and cheese?"

She turned her head from the pot and glared at me. "Wine and cheese? Wine and fucking cheese?"

I nodded.

"Wine and fucking cheese?"

"It's called a chemo party. They're all the rage."

"What in that demented queer brain of yours would make you think I want Joe here smoking his smelly cigars while I am puking my guts up?"

"He promised to not smoke. And…to be honest, I didn't think it was going to be this bad."

She looked up at me, her face splotchy and red and her nose running, and she flipped me the bird. "What would you fucking know about chemo?"

"Only what I see in the movies. And I mean movies like *Love Story* and *Beaches*. I wasn't talking about *The Exorcist*."

"You're an ass. A total ass."

"But I'm an ass who'll sit next to you while you vomit. *That* kind of ass is few and far between, my little pea-soup spewing devil child. Come on…we'll get you down on the couch."

She groaned, but she was at a lull in her vomit session, and she did climb out of bed, put on her robe and shuffle down to the couch. My plan was working. Not that it was much of a plan. I had just been reading all this holistic healing crap. Two things jumped out at me. People who have something to fight for live longer, and people who pray and are prayed for live longer, too. I knew if I told her any of this, she would say I was full of shit, so I kept it to myself but said the rosary for her every morning. And decided angry was a less passive emotion.

The doorbell rang, and I went to the foyer.

"Mikey!" Joe clapped me on the back when I opened the door. He has this heterosexual male tendency to give other men nicknames. So Michael becomes Mikey or Mikey Boy, and Noah goes by Champ. He called Lily's last boyfriend Bob-oh.

I ushered Joe into the living room.

"Jesus H. Christ, you look like crap!" he said to Lily, who was sitting down in a large leather lounge chair that had once been Spawn's favorite.

"One more word about my appearance, and I swear you won't leave here with your testicles."

"You still have your hair."

"For about ten days. Then it all goes bye-bye."

"Won't have to shave your legs."

"Gee, thanks, Joe. I'm sure that's a big plus to chemo. As it is I only shave when I think I might be having sex.

And somehow, the whole I-have-cancer thing isn't exactly first-date material."

"Eh," Joe said, waving his hand. "You were never first-date material. Ever. Too opinionated. You scare men."

She put the pot down on the floor. "I *scare* men! I *scare* men?"

"You heard me. Frighten off every guy in the tri-state area."

I went to get him a beer. My plan was working perfectly. You can't think about giving up when you're pissed. I came back with the beer, and she was midrant. I walked in on, "And I'll tell you another thing, you asshole..."

Then the doorbell rang. She turned her wrath on me. "Who else did you invite, dickhead?"

"Ellie."

"Ellie?"

"What, is there an echo?"

I went and opened the door and ushered her in. Whereas Lily scared off guys, Ellie was a magnet for lots and lots of first dates. Usually weirdos—like the guy who stole all her spoons after she took him home for the night. Not forks. Not knives. Spoons. We were stirring our coffee with pencils in her apartment for a year.

She hugged me when she came in and whispered in my ear, "I promise not to cry."

I hugged her back and led her into the living room.

"Lily...you look great!" Ellie said and went over to the couch and leaned down and hugged her.

"God, you're an awful liar."

"All right. So this isn't your best look. But remember

your eighties hair? Remember leg warmers? Remember…God, the entire eighties decade was a disaster. I consider the blotchy thing a phase, like all of that. Your eyes are the window to your soul and yours are still the same beautiful blue."

"God, all right. Hear this," Lily laughed. "In addition to the No Crying rule, I am instituting the No Maudlin Sentiment rule. I mean, window to the soul. Come off it."

I went to the kitchen and returned with wine, cheese and another beer for Joe.

"So when are you coming back into the office?" Joe asked. "Not that you're in any danger of losing your column."

"First of all, I have never seen why, in the age of e-mail, I ever have to show up at the office."

"Face time. Everybody needs some face time."

"I could do without seeing your face," she snapped.

I leaned back in my chair, very self-satisfied. This was my most brilliant plan yet. The more she fought, the better off she would be.

Ellie ran a hand through her hair. She was pushing forty-five but still looked like a teen refugee from the circus with her flaming hair and "boho" clothing. "So…you want to hear about my latest boyfriend?"

Lily rolled her eyes. "Do we have to?"

"Yes. Now this guy is it. Name's Ken. First of all, he's the first guy in like a year that I've met who doesn't live with his mother."

"Well, sounds like a winner then," Joe said. "You should marry him."

"Thinking about it," Ellie replied. She never got how sarcastic Joe was. "But…well…you know how I have this thing about rats?"

Lily nodded. In fact, Ellie had a raging, screaming full-blown phobia of rodents. Whenever they even appeared on television, like on *Survivor,* she had to be sedated. Or at least she had to change the channel.

"He has a pet rat."

Joe shook his head. "I knew that was coming."

"So, you know, he's very attached to Albert. And so we're trying to figure this all out. I mean, I'd move in with him. He has a better apartment than me. But…it's too gross to contemplate. I even tried hypnosis to get over my fear, but I just can't go within fifty feet of that rat."

"Well, the last guy I dated," Lily said, "took out a calculator to figure out how to split the bill at the restaurant."

"Which guy was that?" Joe asked.

"The doctor."

"A friggin' doctor and he's splitting the bill?" Ellie shrieked. "And I thought I had it bad."

"I know. I'd be better off dating Michael for all the action I'm getting. And now… You think while bald I'll meet anyone?"

"Sure. You should try a Twelve-Step program. I met a ton of men in A.A.," Ellie said.

Joe looked at her as she had her wineglass raised. "But you're not an alcoholic."

"I know. But men fresh into the program? They make great dates. They're getting all spiritual."

"Nothing like starting off in an honest relationship," Lily cracked.

We laughed and talked about old times. Ellie and I polished off a bottle of wine, and Joe had another beer. Lily looked tired.

"Hate to kick you out, guys, but my days of partying until dawn are over. At least tonight they are."

Joe rose and went over to kiss the top of her head. "Hang in there, kiddo."

Ellie stood and wrapped her fuzzy red scarf around her neck. "Best chemo party I've ever been to. I'll see if Ken has a brother."

"No, that's okay."

I walked Joe and Ellie to the door. "Thanks, guys," I whispered.

Joe gave me a wink, and Ellie hugged me.

Walking back into the living room, I ducked to avoid a throw pillow Lily hurled from the couch.

"What?"

"Michael, did it ever occur to you that I might want a little privacy as I puke my guts up and stumble around in old nightgowns?"

"No. You were the woman who entered the wet T-shirt contest the time you wrote a story on spring break. You were the woman who told the doctors to hold a mirror up to…you know where so we could both see Noah being born. You used to breastfeed in a way to *invite* conflict, as if you were just *waiting* for someone to give you shit about an exposed nipple. Privacy? I don't think so."

"I draw the line at puke."

"Personally, I think their visit did you a world of good. You have color in your cheeks now."

She glared at me. "Next time you have a hangover…I'm sticking anchovies on your pillow."

I was thrilled. Anger, I was sure, would keep her fighting.

I went to check on Noah after I settled Lily in with a movie. He was still awake and staring at the ceiling.

"What's up, kiddo?"

"I don't get this chemo thing."

"What about it?"

"Mom gets sick because the chemicals make her sick."

"Sort of. The chemicals that make her better also make her sick."

"That makes no sense."

"I know."

"Cancer makes no sense. Why did God make it? It kills people."

Damn, kids really come up with the Big Questions.

"Sure, sometimes. But you know when the Yanks are down at the bottom of the ninth?"

"Uh-huh."

"What do I tell you?"

"It ain't over until the fat lady sings."

"And what does that mean?"

"You told me, 'Anything can happen.'"

"Right. So we never give up."

"Right, Uncle Michael. Never."

"Okay then. So…" I took a big breath. "You know how your Mom has cancer?"

"Uh-huh?"

"Well, no matter how sick she is, we can't give up. Being sick actually means the drugs are doing what they're supposed to."

"Okay." I saw his eyes go dead. Maybe I hadn't noticed before how he steeled himself for bad news each time she went to her doctor's appointments lately.

His eyes welled up, and he turned his little face away from me.

"It's okay to cry, Noah. We can be scared. We can. But we have to keep praying that she gets well. And soon!" I tousled his hair, hoping to lure him out of whatever grim path he was skipping down.

"Tell me the truth. Is Mom going to die?"

"We all die someday, Noah."

"You always say that."

"It's always true."

"Is she going to die *soon?*"

"I could walk out of my apartment and get hit by a bus tomorrow, Noah. We don't know when we're going to die. Only God knows. It's like the great Lottery in the Sky. When it's your number, it's your number."

"You always say that, too." Noah turned back to look me in the eyes, and a tear balanced in the outer corner of his eye and finally trickled down his freckled cheeks.

"Uncle Michael?" he whispered.

"Yes, Sweetie."

"No matter what, will you be my uncle forever?"

"No matter what."

"Cross your heart, hope to die, stick a thousand needles in your eye?"

"Wow. A thousand needles. You know how I hate pain." I mock-shuddered. "I'm really wimpy that way."

He giggled.

"I love you, Noah."

"I love you, too, Uncle Michael."

I turned out the light and went downstairs to clean up after the chemo party.

I read. I worked on my book—my editor was pushing me to finish it before March first. When I went back to check on Noah, I saw he had kicked off all the covers, and I once again pulled them up under his chin and kissed him on the forehead. The rosary beads I'd given him were in his hand. Lily told me he slept with them under his pillow.

Noah had saved me from myself seven years ago on a snowy night. I swore a thousand needles in my eye that whatever happened he would not be alone.

15

Sisters
by Lily Waters

I used to go to parties, in my vain and glorious twenties, and look around the room and see each woman as competition. Each woman was shorter or thinner, fatter or had bad hair—compared to me. Or they were taller and more glamorous. Maybe they dressed cheaply or wore their makeup wrong. Their eyeliner wasn't drawn on quite right. Or they threw themselves at men and made fools of themselves. Whatever their faults, I spotted them. Whatever mine were, I obsessed over them. I was the center of my own universe. I saw all of us women in some sort of competition for men. If I walked into a room dressed sexy and felt all eyes upon me, I won. If I walked in overdressed or underdressed, or with my perm frizzed out, I lost. Maybe I am too

young. I missed the bra-burning women's rights
era. Other women weren't my sisters. They were
the enemy.

Now I go to parties and feel the irony. The perm
is gone. So is my hair. I'm bald. Even my eyebrows
are gone. So there's no comparing me to them anymore. If the other women in the room *have* hair,
they're beating me. But, still, now I look around,
now that I have breast cancer, and I silently count
to eight. I look around the room, thinking one, two,
three, four...seven, eight...is she the one? A statis-
tic of one in eight women getting breast cancer? Is
she my sister? Is she going to find out that she has
a lump one day and the lump is cancer and watch
her world turn upside down because of this disease?

Even more ironic is that I share my life, as my
readers know, with my best friend, who is a gorgeous man—but gay. Besides the fact that his culinary skills save my children from starvation, he is
whom I choose to walk through this journey with.
All that competition to end up sitting on the bench.

I have also chosen to walk through this journey
with my readers, and so this is one of the more difficult columns I have ever had to write. For you see,
the roulette wheel has spun, and number eight has
come up for me. I have breast cancer.

My readers have been there for me through bad
dates, and even a stalker, through bad hair days, and
a husband caught cheating. And this time I expect
it to be no different. But this time I am more aware
that I may not survive, and that even if I do, some
of my sisters will not. I do not want these sisters. I
want to, in some strange way, go back in time to

frizzy perms and flirtations across the room, not this. Not one in eight contracting breast cancer. Not time running out.

For every reader who wants to send me a get-well card and flowers and scarves and books, I ask that instead you donate one dollar to research. One dollar to make sure this sisterhood is ended…and I can go back to hating my competition.

16

Lily

Chemotherapy is chemical warfare. You hope the chemicals, the same poisons that make your hair fall out and make you vomit and feel so tired even your eyelashes hurt, win. You hope your body loses.

In the beginning, Michael came with me to each session and held my hand as they started my I.V., and we watched the steady drip snake its way into my arm. However, after a couple of sessions, I decided I was a big enough girl to be dropped off.

"I'll call you on your cell when you can pick me up."

"You sure you're okay alone?"

"Yeah."

The cancer center where I get my treatment lines up lounge chairs in rooms. They want you to be comfortable for your chemical warfare. Our doctors tell us to bring personal CD players and music to relax to or music that will help us fight. They are into imagery. They tell us to picture Pac-Man gangs eating the bad cells, or little soldiers going to war. I found the whole idea preposterous, as if having a video game in my body would help me beat cancer. But I tell myself I will do whatever they tell me. If a fucking Pac-Man improves my odds, then bring on the little disembodied eating head that makes that weird noise as he munches away the cancer.

Usually, at the treatment place, I got my own cubicle-type room, with my very own lounge chair. Nurses brought Michael sodas and typical hospital snacks—crackers. It's a regular party. But when I went for my third chemo treatment, the reception area was wall-to-wall bald people, and they asked if I would share a room.

My roomie for the day was an attractive, bald (what else?) man. The minute he grinned, I liked him, as he had dimples like great chasms in his cheeks and pale blue eyes. I suppose the dimples would have been handsome if he had hair, but without hair or eyebrows, they sort of made him look like a happy Kewpie doll. Adorable.

"Pete Bartlett," he said, sticking out the hand that didn't have chemo traveling into its veins.

"Lily Waters." I smiled.

"Beautiful name."

"Thanks."

The nurse settled me into my lounge chair and asked if I wanted a blanket, which I did. Chemotherapy alternates between making me have chills and making me feel as if I am on fire. I asked her for an ice pack as long as she was getting the blanket, covering both my bases so I wouldn't have to bother her again. She busied herself preparing my poisons, and I didn't even blink when she poked for a vein. I used to break out in a cold sweat at the thought of needles. Cancer changes that. No flinching. It's like boot camp for the medically chicken.

The nurse left after reminding me I could buzz her if I needed anything. She smiled at me. I usually have Carol, a real sweetie pie, but I guessed she was off. This nurse was also nice, efficient. She looked at my chart, and I tried to decide what she thought as she read it. Will I beat it or not? Then I banished the thought from my mind and tried to picture a Pac-Man.

After she left, Peter turned his head in my direction, "Mind if I ask what kind of cancer you have?"

"No. We're part of the same club, aren't we? I have breast cancer."

"I'm sorry. That really sucks. And I'm sorry I said I'm sorry. I hate when people say that to me. Like…what? They caused it?"

"I hate that, too. And it does suck, doesn't it? How about you?"

"Hodgkins. This is my last treatment."

"Congratulations, graduate. You'll have hair in no time. Unless, of course, you are actually a bald man. Then you'll just get eyebrows."

He laughed. "No. I usually have hair."

"I don't." My bald head was wrapped in the Hermés scarf from Michael.

He looked at me, and then I laughed. "No, I'm not really bald."

"You had me worried there." He grinned at me.

"So your last treatment…. You'll be fine. Hodgkins. Very curable."

"You know," he smiled, "let's talk about something else. Like you have an unlimited budget and you can go on vacation anywhere in the world, so where would you go?"

"Disneyworld."

"Really?"

"No. I hate that little mouse. Umm, no one ever asked me this before. Okay, I guess Bali."

"Bali."

"No, Ireland. Ireland, definitely. A fishing village in Ireland. Get lost and write for a while."

"Are you a writer?"

I nodded. I felt hot and put the icepack on the back of my neck. "I write a column. For the *Tribune*."

"Wait a minute…." He leaned back and grinned. "Even with that scarf on I recognize you from your picture. Lily Waters. Now I know why your name sounded familiar to me. I've read your column before. There was one about…what the hell was it? Oh yeah, there was one about your childhood crush that I thought was really funny. The David Cassidy column."

"Yeah. Androgynous little guy. Who can explain childhood crushes? Glad you liked it. What do you do?"

"I'm a teacher."

"What do you teach?"

"High school math."

"Math?"

"I know. I'm a geek. That was me in school—nerdy guy. Pocket protector, the whole nine yards."

"That's hard to picture. Even bald you're cute."

His eyes welled up momentarily. I would have missed it, but I was looking at him closely. When you have cancer, you sort of feel like this asexual pinhead. Bald on top, dead below the waist. Who will want me? All that.

"Thank you. I'm cuter with hair, believe me. I could even stand being bald, but I'd like eyelashes again. And eyebrows."

"Me, too." I laughed. "I will never ever again bitch about plucking my eyebrows." I felt less asexual myself being near him. He was warm and charming, and his voice was DJ-smooth. Deep. "So I still don't believe you were a geek."

"Yup. The worst. I even had Coke-bottle glasses until I got contacts. I wore anything hanging in my closet. Never cared about cool. I cared about science and math. Then I went through this hormonal revolution and started liking girls, starting with my lab partner, but she liked the quarterback of the football team."

"Fool. Those guys go to pot after a while. It's the geeks who later rule the world."

"I agree. But I realized girls cared about whether or not you had a pocket protector and dorky pants. I took a good look at my wardrobe. My haircut—can you say buzz cut?—I grew it out again, not that you can tell…but I do look better with hair. Over time, I got less geeky but still loved science and math, and now I teach math. And the best part is nearly every kid comes to my class hating math and thinking the class is going to be the worst thing they've ever taken…and I make it fun."

"I wish my daughter had you."

"Oh…" He looked at my left hand. "How many kids do you have?"

"Two. Tara is in high school, and Noah is seven. He's in second grade. I'm divorced."

He smiled and looked relieved. About the divorced part. "I'm sorry. It must be tough on your kids, you having cancer. Even my students…they worry over me and fuss over me. And some of them seem angry with me, as if they're mad I'm making them think about death. It's complicated with kids. But they're honest, too, so in a way that's less complicated than adults who seem at a loss for what to say so they avoid me."

I sighed. I related all too well. A couple of acquaintances disappeared when I got cancer. It was as if I was a living, breathing example of their own mortality and they wanted to avoid me at all costs. People think, "My friends would never do that to me." But Carol, my regular nurse, told me it happens all the time.

I looked at the Kewpie cutie next to me. "Anyone who would avoid you is an idiot, Peter."

"I try to tell myself that."

We spent the rest of our chemotherapy bonding time talking about our lives. Who we were. It was as if our baldness stripped us of any need to be false with each other. We talked about God and whether we were angry at him. We talked about loneliness. We talked a little about death, and chemo.

"You know," he said, "I have three students in my classes I think are bulimics. I hear the rumors about them, and they have some telltale signs. I went to talk to the school counselor about them—they need help. And sometimes, when I am throwing up, I cannot imagine the self-loathing that must cause you to *want* to make yourself throw up."

"I know. That whole excessive saliva thing. The waves of nausea. Whoever coined the term 'waves' knew what he or she was talking about. It is like waves crashing over you."

"God, it's the worst."

I looked across at him. Here was a man I could talk about puking with, for God's sake. Most of my dates never made it past the "What do you do for a living?" stage. The two kids scared them off. Or the fact that I am opinionated. And then once I got cancer, forget it.

When we were both finished with treatment, he stood up. "Can I take you to dinner sometime, Lily? I really can't believe I'm saying this but…I enjoyed chemo today." His dimples deepened.

My heartbeat quickened, with dread, not happiness. He hadn't yet figured it out, what had slowly dawned on me. "I can't, Peter. Though Lord knows I would love to. I really, really would." I faltered.

"So why not?"

"You're going to get better, Peter. Hodgkins is the good cancer. I mean, if you have to get cancer, that's the one to get."

"Remind me to bet the lottery. Must have been my lucky day when I found the lump under my collarbone."

I laughed. "I don't mean it that way. I just mean, I guess, that right now I have this bit of a question mark. I'm not sure what's going to happen to me."

"You're going to get well."

I shook my head and shrugged my shoulders.

"Don't think that." He took my hand. "Come on. There really is something to the power of thinking positive."

"Yeah. I mean, I'm fighting, but I'm sort of mentally putting my house in order, you know."

"Have the doctors told you that it's bad?"

"Not in so many words, but yes. And as much as I would love to go to dinner with you...and believe me, my tolerance for bullshit went out the window when I got sick—oh, who am I kidding? I've never had a high tolerance for B.S.—so I won't lie to you. I would love to kiss you." I touched his other hand and felt my stomach lurch with lust—one thing, apparently, chemo hadn't killed. "What we shared today was really cathartic for me. It was special. And maybe if I really do get well I'll call you. But if we go out for dinner, right now, I mean sometime soon, I can tell where this would head."

"So can I," he whispered.

"And you see...you'd be one more room in my house I would have to put in order. One more person I would grow to adore I might have to say goodbye to. So I can't. Cancer pretty much rearranged my life."

I moved closer to him and kissed him on the lips. As kisses go, I ranked it in my top three.

He stepped back, breathless. "God…Lily, I can handle a relationship with you even though you're sick. Life *is* short. Cancer teaches you that in spades. Come on, let me take you out."

"I can't."

He sighed. "Then just get better. I'll expect a call from you when your hair's grown back and you feel great and you've beaten this. I teach at St. Vincent's. Call me. And don't say anything else. I have to believe you're going to call me or right now I'm going to fall apart."

"Okay, Peter. I'll call you." I turned to go, and I felt a surge of tears. I knew I was going to sob, and I wanted my exit to be graceful, so I ran down the hall. I know he cried, but not half as bad as I did. When I got into the car with Michael, I couldn't even speak.

"You'll tell me later, right?" He knows me so well.

I nodded.

"Then put your head down on my lap and have a good cry." He opened the glove box and handed me a tissue. "Just cry, Lily. Get it out."

"Shit…" I felt the tears drowning me.

"Are you blowing your nose on my jeans? Ever since you got cancer, it's like we're in this constant body fluid stage. Puke, snot. It's gross."

I slapped his leg. "Shut up or I really will blow my nose on your leg."

"That's so seductive."

I rolled my eyes. "You really drive me crazy, you know."

"I know. That's my job."

I shut my eyes and thought of Pete. The connection with him was palpable. Maybe a date with a bald man with no eyebrows wouldn't be such a bad idea after all.

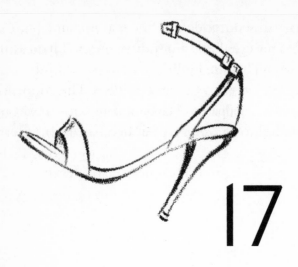

17

Michael

It's hard to know exactly when Lily started giving up. I think it was piece by piece, day by day. Sometimes, Noah would wrap his arms around her, and she would breathe in that heavenly child scent and for moments or hours, she would fight. I could see it in her eyes. Other days, throwing up on a towel because she couldn't reach the toilet, the indignity of being too weak and too tired to even wipe her nose when she cried, I saw the light go out. But she was changed after her third chemotherapy treatment. I couldn't put my finger on it, but I think it was simply the resignation.

Resignation has a weary connotation, and in Lily's case, that simply wasn't so. Or maybe she was weary at first, but in its place grew grace. She had a quality about her that I could not define. She was no saint, but Catholic that I am, I think in terms of grace. Lily was filled with serenity and dignity, and motherhood stopped being about cleaning up dirty dishes and driving the carpool every morning and became a religion. It all meant more to her. But I sensed it was because she believed she was leaving us. That she was losing the fight. So, even as Lily changed into this calmer person, less frenetic, less bitchy, less difficult, we fought more than we ever had before.

Our relationship, for twenty years, had been built on acceptance. The last time we fought with regularity was at the height of the AIDS crisis. I had refused to get tested. And I had refused to use condoms.

After our friendship weathered that, life was still life. It threw us curveballs. I started my novel a dozen times, only to give up when the memories became too painful. I'm only on track with it now, two decades after the events that changed me. She was the one to get me to write about it.

"You never talk about the assault."
I shrugged. "There's not much to talk about."
"Bullshit."
"Look, you're not a guy."
"So because I don't have a penis means I can't understand?"
We were sitting in our favorite watering hole, talking about my latest round of writer's block. I hate that she's never had writer's block. But was it any wonder? She was

never at a loss for words. She always had something to say—whether I and the rest of the world wanted to hear it or not. And she had to have the last word.

"A penis would be helpful."

"You are so full of crap."

"I'm not. Look, what do you think guys talk about in the locker room?"

"Women."

"I know. But in what way? How graphic?"

Lily pushed back a stray curl and raised her shoulders in an I-don't-know gesture. "Tits. Ass. Who put out. I don't know."

"Well, it can get pretty intense in there. They talk about women in ways that make porno seem buttoned-up. Like they're things. No—worse. Like they're holes. A mouth, a...well, you get the idea. For insertion. And nothing more. And in this hypersexed locker room environment, there is nothing worse than a guy being gay. It's unheard of. On the collegiate level—at the level I was playing, where some of those guys were drafted by the majors—it just was beyond unacceptable. It was a crime. It was like I committed an act of betrayal."

Lily lifted her martini and sipped. Put it down and shook her head. "By you saying that, you are somehow justifying what they did to you, as if you did something so wrong you deserved that."

"No. I'm not justifying it. I just guess I understand in a way."

"You know, Michael, we spend a lot of time talking about being honest in our writing. A lot of time. And

I think the reason you have writer's block is that by not writing about what happened and locking it up inside—and instead writing about just hints of yourself—that you're blocking your whole creative side."

I raised my hand in the air. "Paging Dr. Freud…. What a load of pseudointellectual bull-crap."

"It isn't."

"So are writers only meant to write memoirs?"

"No. Writing is like a hall of mirrors. There are pieces of you there, but it's all distorted in the funhouse glass until readers don't know what's you and what's fiction. But the emotions, the reality, the blood of what's on the page, that has to come from you, Michael. And the longer you hide behind that locker room door, the longer you'll be blocked."

"You know nothing about my problems."

"Suit yourself, Gay Boy. But I bet you know I'm right."

Of course, she knew a lot more than I gave her credit for. I didn't tell her—or my agent—but it hit me like a bolt of lightning that what Lily was telling me was Writing 101. My creative writing professors in college had always demanded something of you in the writing. Feelings. So I went back to the assault, and I started writing. And I found that writing about Sam freed me to really say what happened.

The whole novel is like a love letter to Lily. It's not about her at all, but the novel wouldn't exist without her prodding.

God, our history went on and on. She couldn't give

up, because we were each too much a part of the other. We even weathered Spawn. She married David, which was a huge mistake, though I tried to like him despite his smug college-professor smirk. I introduced them— not to have them date or anything, but just casually at an English department function. He left soon after for greener pastures at NYU—a more prestigious university. In the adage of "publish or perish," he was kicking ass with several pieces in literary journals and a piece in the *New Yorker.*

Theirs was an intense, fast courtship—and sex was a big part of it. There was a combustible attraction between them.

Then Lily had Tara. A kid changes a marriage and changes a friendship—but we still talked as if nothing had changed, because for us, everything had changed but the friendship at our core. When she got pregnant with Noah, she had to be on bed rest for a few weeks. And then of course Spawn left her. Because, for him, not being the center of her universe was unacceptable. When he left, it almost killed her.

Funny to hear that expression now. Cancer puts a lot of things in perspective.

Anyway, I was convinced nothing could kill her if she could survive Spawn's abandonment.

But this was different, and by the third chemo treatment, even the way she talked about it had gotten more resolved to the fact that she would not be there to watch Noah grow up.

"Will you make sure he doesn't forget me?" she asked

one night. We were lying in her king-size bed. She had a big soup pot next to her in case she needed to throw up in a hurry. She had an ice pack on the back of her neck and one on her forehead.

"Shut up! Because if you think I won't bitch-slap you now that you have cancer, you're wrong. Stop talking like that."

"Michael, I need you to be the one person on this earth I can be entirely honest with. It's truly exhausting for me to have to keep up this pretense that I am definitely going to live. I am buying time. Borrowed time. I lie here every night and try to figure out what I am going to do to get these kids ready for life without me. And every time you deny me the chance to be honest, I just—" She didn't finish her sentence but took a tissue I offered her.

"I believe in miracles."

"I don't, damn you."

"Miracles aren't about kneeling in a church, or weeping statues, Lily. Miracles just happen. They're part of the plan."

"Whose plan?"

"The Big Man's."

She turned her head to face me. Pillow talk without the sex. I was sleeping over so I could take Noah to my mother's for brunch the next day. The ice pack slid off to the side. Her nose was running. Her face was blotchy.

"See, that's where I have a problem. Because if miracles are part of the Big Man's plan, then me being sick is also a part of it. I mean, okay, into each life a little rain must fall. People get cancer, so why not me? But damn it, why me? When I'm a single mother? Where's the goddamn plan in that?"

"I ask the Big Man that every night, Lil. But you still have to believe. What happened to Pac-Man and visualization?"

"I'm still doing my internal video game."

"But you're doing it thinking you're going to lose. What if you did it thinking you could win? That you could get the high score on the Pac-Man machine of life."

"Michael, that's the worst pep talk I have ever heard in my life."

"I've heard worse."

"No you haven't."

"Yes, I have. I played baseball in college, remember. I had coaches who majored in cliché. One for the Gipper and all that."

"You still didn't answer me. Will you make sure he doesn't forget me?"

"Lily, stop it. Noah is not going to forget you." My voice rose. I stopped looking at her and stared up at the ceiling. "You're his *mother*. And you're not going anywhere."

"But he will forget me. I mean, he won't forget me because he'll have pictures and memories, but after a while, I mean a long while, he will. Like when he's fifteen or twenty-five, or when he's getting married, he'll try to remember what I smelled like, my voice, how it felt to have me hug him, and he'll realize that I'm fading. That the pictures and videos are vivid, but what's in his heart is more like a whisper."

"You're larger than life. Trust me. First of all, how could he forget all of the horrible meals you've subjected him to? Or the Halloween costumes you made him—never store-bought? I mean, what kid is going to forget the year his mother made him a shark costume, complete with the world's biggest cardboard fin? Or the lobster costume when he was obsessed with crustaceans? And what about how you've never missed a Little League game? All this while Spawn is fucking the Child Bride and living in London. You were—are—there for him, Lily, and he will hold onto that forever. Along with all the new memories. Because I intend to dance with you at his wedding."

"David can't raise them."

"No. He can't."

"My parents are both dead. I have a cousin who's a lush in California whom I haven't seen in fifteen years."

"And you're an only child. Which, frankly, beats the god-awful sister I have."

"That leaves you, you know."

"Please…I will always be here for them, you know that."

"But you hear what I'm saying."

"I hear you. But they belong with family."

"*You're* their family. We'll table this for now. To be discussed in the near future."

"Tabled. Now what do you say we pop in a video of Vivian Leigh in *Waterloo Bridge*, bawl our eyes out and mutually swoon over the late, great and very beautiful Robert Taylor."

"Now there's another man we can agree on."

"Certainly. Not like that little boy-toy actor you like. Orlando Bloom."

"Please. He is very sexy."

"You need to like some real men."

"I won't even touch that one, Michael."

"Want some popcorn?" I sat up.

"Couldn't keep it down."

"Warm ginger ale?"

"Sounds heavenly."

I went downstairs to get her some ginger ale and to get the video. The house was quiet. Tara was sleeping at her girlfriend Jody's house, and Noah was long since asleep. I found myself staring out at the lawn from the kitchen window. We'd had a snowstorm two days earlier, and everything still looked pristine out in the 'burbs. For some reason, the sight of the snow, the quiet house, the little stained-glass suncatchers Noah and Lily made and baked in the toaster oven and stuck with suction cups to the window, I felt this lurch of emotion inside of me and I started to cry. I slid down to the floor and sobbed into my knees for a good ten minutes. The thought that she spent nights wondering if Noah would forget her, if she would become this faded ghost in our hearts, destroyed me.

I collected myself, rinsed my face with some cold water, wiped my eyes in her ratty pale blue dish towel, and went back upstairs with soda and the movie. In hindsight, it was a bad choice. At first, we sighed over Robert Taylor as the dashing Roy. He swept Vivian

Leigh, as the young ballerina, right off her feet. Every glance between them was straight out of old Hollywood. Roy was dreamy; she was the innocent. By the end of the four-hankie sobfest, Vivian Leigh's character of Myra had given up on life. She walked in a trance, along Waterloo Bridge, dazed by her own heartache. For the second time that night, I cried. Myra died right there on the bridge. But Roy had a good-luck charm from Myra in his pocket, and there he was, thirty years later, standing on Waterloo Bridge remembering everything about her. It was as if Myra was still alive. Myra. Lily. Was there any doubt she would stay in our hearts?

18

Curveball
An excerpt from a novel by Michael Angelo

Sam stirred. He wondered if he was seeing things. A light was on in the locker room and someone was standing over him.

He tried to think back to what had happened, but in actuality, all he could think of was his pain. Breathing hurt, his face hurt, and he felt like he was going to puke from swallowing blood. He rolled onto his side and retched.

His eyes were nearly swollen shut, and he was trying to tell his limbs to move, to tell his arms to cover his face, to defend himself from this figure standing over him. He wondered if it was Charlie, back to finish the job. Back to kill him.

The figure bent down, and he heard the voice of his coach, Carl Ditford. Coach Carl.

"Hey there, Sam."

Sam couldn't speak. He tried to open his mouth, but found he couldn't.

"Son…" Coach Carl said, his voice soft, much quieter than during practice session when his Texas twang barked across the field. "Seems you had a bit of a disagreement with the boys."

"Mmm." Sam managed to utter a sound.

Still softly, only now with a threat in the whisper, Coach Carl said, "Well, it's a shame you didn't see anything. Didn't see who hit you. Didn't see nothin'. Shame. Boys will be boys, Sam. Real boys, that is. And if you want an ambulance, you better swear on your mama's life that you didn't see nothin'."

"Mmm," was all Sam could say. His heart pounded. He could feel the blood spewing from his nose in time with his pulse.

"You're gonna have to do better than that. Was that a yes? Blink your eyes once for yes. Slowly. So I can see."

With every bit of himself, every scrap of fight left in him, Sam wanted to live and so, with difficulty, he opened his eyes as wide as they would go—not much more than slits. And then shut them. He blinked. Once.

Coach Carl slapped him—hard—on the shoulder. "Good little faggot. I'll call you an ambulance now." He stood up, then spat on Sam before he turned on his lizard skin cowboy boot heels and walked out of the locker room, and, Sam prayed, called an ambulance.

19

Lily

While it wasn't "time yet," I discussed with Dr. Morris how, if it got really bad, I wanted to die at home. I had become a walking medical dictionary. Ductal, in situ, carcinoma…invasive, stage four, the words could spill out of me at will. I told Dr. Morris that I would let him know when I'd had enough treatment—or he would. When and if fighting became pointless, I would have hospice care at home. I was planning ahead, which was never my strong suit. But spontaneous and cancer didn't seem to be two words that sat well together. So next I visited two lawyers.

The first lawyer was my family attorney, Harry Conklin, a sweetheart of a guy who'd known me since my father died and we had to settle the estate. Harry always wore bow ties to the office. He possessed quite a collection, including a light-up one for Christmas, one with orange pumpkins for Halloween and a red, white and blue one for the Fourth of July. Good lawyer jokes abound—you know the ones about how they're all sharks, but Harry reminded me of the kind of lawyer you'd picture in a sleepy, little town. Sort of like Andy Griffith as Matlock, minus the Southern drawl.

As soon as I got sick, I had contacted him. Harry drew up a durable power of attorney, naming Michael, of course. I also told him I wanted to come back to discuss my estate, which amounted to a house with a leaky roof, a dog that snored and two children—one a petulant teen that *I* sometimes wondered if I wanted to take care of.

Without telling anyone, after a month of chemo, I had an appointment with Harry to draw up a will. The children would have to go to David, he had said over the phone, but I wanted to name Michael their legal guardian anyway. There was always a chance Spawn wouldn't want them. I considered it, actually, more than a chance. Because though David might, in his narcissistic heart, actually love his kids, Child Bride did not.

But in my heart, I knew my wishes aside, I probably didn't stand much legal chance of naming Michael. Still, I showed up to my appointment with the Bow Tie King, determined to make him see it my way.

"Lily," Harry hugged me tightly and ushered me into his office, which had that moneyed "clubby" feel of rich burgundy leather, brass and a banker's lamp on his desk casting a soft green glow.

I settled into a leather chair that seemed to swallow me up amidst its two massive arms, and I smiled at him.

"Harry...the cancer's kicking my ass. Now I don't want you getting all blubbery on me. I'm here because I want a living will. I do not want to be hooked up on machines should things go terribly wrong."

I watched him remove his glasses in a tired gesture and rub his eyes. My father had been the hard-drinking sort who loved his family and hated lawyers, doctors and priests. But he had trusted Harry. Behind the goofy bow ties was a man who cared, and a very smart lawyer to boot. Yale.

"Lily, I'm very, very sorry." He put his glasses back on. "Is it...bad? Listen to me. When is cancer good? How are you doing, you know, considering."

Considering. It's such a cancer word. Considering you've got cancer cells running amok. Considering there's this chance you could die. "All things considered, I'm okay. And yes it is bad, so can you draw up a living will?"

"Of course. Now..." He was all business, pulling out a yellow pad to take notes on. "I hate to be so...morbid, but have you thought about how long...? The timing? You see, we can write up a do not resuscitate order, a DNR. That means that if you, say, had a massive heart attack during surgery or stopped breathing, they wouldn't do anything to prolong your life, no extraordinary measures. No CPR. No tubes, no life-saving. And considering your age—that you're young and not some ninety-year-old in a nursing home—you'd have to be pretty sick before they would honor it. Still you're sure you want that?"

"Absolutely."

"Okay, then. There's a second part to this. Let's suppose you slipped into a coma, but you were still hanging in there. Would you want them to not feed you? Would you want them to wait a period of time, say two weeks, before discontinuing feeding or life support? Because even with a DNR, suppose you collapsed at a store. The ambulance comes and they don't know you have a DNR, it's conceivable you could end up on life support even with the DNR, you follow?"

"I follow."

"So you need to decide what's a good time to wait?"

"Like two weeks and then pull the plug?"

"Yes." He took off his glasses again and rubbed his eyes. I saw a tremble in his hand.

"Two weeks sounds good."

"Don't be flippant. Think about it." Glasses back on, a return to business.

"Two weeks. That's reasonable. Gives people time to gather at my deathbed, say their goodbyes. Maybe my ex-husband will even grovel at my bedside. I like it. Two weeks."

"All right, then. Two weeks."

He put down his pen. "I hope you don't have to use this, Lily, but I guess you're here because realistically you might. I take it you're naming your friend Michael again."

"Yes, Harry. I want him as executor of the will. Now

I know I had a sort of basic will once I became a single parent. But, you know, I never really thought I might *need* it. You know? I mean, it was all this theoretical crap. So I want to make a couple of changes to what I originally had. I want to leave Michael my piano. Tara quit taking lessons, and Michael loves it. I catch him sitting down to play once in a while. But now I need to know something…"

"Shoot."

"I don't want my children's father to get them if I die."

"Why?"

"This isn't a 'woman scorned' kind of thing. He ended up marrying that young student he was seeing, and they have an infant now. She's just a child, herself, really. Not too much older than Tara. And to be honest the children no longer get phone calls, Christmas cards, nothing. He and his wife have a new life, and my children are not part of it. The kids would never want to leave the U.S., their friends, the life they have, to go to England. And to be honest, when I mentioned, after he left, that I was doing up a will and maybe he should too, he made a fuss about how I couldn't die because he couldn't imagine them full-time."

"Well, we have that in the will, but it's not iron-clad at all. A judge would want them to go to their father."

"Here's the thing, Harry. I want Michael to raise them."

Harry fiddled with his bow tie—a navy blue one with white polka dots.

"Very tough, Lily."

"Yeah, well, I'm in a tough spot, so—"

"What you need, Lily, is a bulldog."

"Hmm?"

"You don't need a gentleman lawyer, you need a hard-ass. You need Jack Tessa. He's the toughest, meanest, orneriest lawyer in Westchester. But he has a soft spot for kids. He'll figure out a way to do what you want and have it airtight. I'll call him and explain a little. Can you meet him next week?"

I nodded. "Thanks, Harry." We both stood, and he walked me to the door. I gave him a hug. He held me a minute longer than he would have if I hadn't just come to tell him I was dying.

So, the next week I found myself in the law offices of Finn, Finn, Smith and Tessa. Jack Tessa was no Matlock. He had on an Italian suit with creases so sharp they seemed to slice the air ahead of him as he walked. His tie was a three-hundred dollar silk Gucci I'd seen in an ad, and he had a Rolex on his wrist that was encrusted with diamonds. He was maybe fifty-five and had the soft tan of a man who gets to the golf courses of Florida a few times a winter. His hair was silver and cut short. His eyes were blue, and they were very, very cold. I decided I would not want to be on the opposite side of the courtroom from Jack W. Tessa, Esquire.

"Harry explained your situation to me a little bit, but I'd really like it if you explained it yourself. This is not going to be easy, especially in light of your friend being a homosexual and the children's father still living."

"I have cancer. Stage four. That's pretty much the toss-in-the-towel stage. I'm receiving chemotherapy and will be in a clinical trial for a new treatment, but for all intents and purposes, Mr. Tessa, you are looking at someone who will likely die of cancer. Everything I am doing is in preparation for that. It's to prepare my children for life without me."

I had decided, the minute I looked into his eyes, that I would play this tough. I would be hard, not some sympathy case. That was the way to play Jack Tessa. He was the kind of man who admired a tough broad. I felt it.

"Go on," he said. Unlike George, he didn't rub his eyes or look away. He stared me down, and I stared back and kept talking.

"My children's father is a deadbeat dad. Plain and simple. He hasn't called them in eight months. He remembers to send his child support sporadically. He has started a new life with a woman who is only ten years older than our fifteen-year-old daughter. He works as a professor in London and makes a decent enough salary with that and royalties from an anthology he edited to support them comfortably, but there is no 'extra' money for the two children he abandoned along with me. When he left, he, to speak bluntly, never looked back."

Jack Tessa nodded almost imperceptibly.

I inhaled and started again. "I have no living relatives except a batty cousin who lives in California. Michael has been the dominant male presence in my children's lives and a surrogate father."

"Your parents are both deceased?"

"My mother died of lung cancer when I was twelve years old. My father died of complications from emphysema five years ago. They were both extremely heavy smokers."

"And so you wish for the children to be raised by your friend, Mr. Michael Angelo."

"Yes." I folded my hands in my lap. Jack Tessa, Esquire, had a way about him that made you wonder where you should put your hands. If I still had hair, I might have nervously played with a strand.

"And Mr. Angelo is an admitted homosexual, and he is of no relation to the children."

I swallowed. When you put it plainly, it didn't sound so good.

"Look, Mr. Tessa, Michael was in the delivery room when Noah was born. He cut the cord while my ex-husband was stuck in a snowstorm…and, I later found out, holed up in a hotel room with his barely-of-age girlfriend. Michael is a prominent professor, educated at NYU, he played baseball in college and continues to be an avid sports fan. He attends Mass every Sunday and every day of Lent. He has taught my children the Our Father and Hail Mary and has taught them right from wrong. He cooks for them and does their laundry. He irons better than I do. When he packs their lunches no detail is overlooked, down to cutting off the crusts. He knows how much Noah weighs, when he lost his first tooth and how Noah throws up when he eats Spaghet-tiOs and drinks milk in combination. Some kind of chemical reaction. And he's brave enough to *clean it up.* He knows my daughter is in the throes of obnoxious adolescence, and he tolerates her excessive moodiness.

He can tell you about her first period because she happened to get it during the seventh-inning stretch of a Yankee game, and he had to handle it himself because I was with Noah at a Cub Scout picnic. In short, there is nothing you or anyone could say that would convince me otherwise that he is the person who should raise my children, and the choice of who he screws has nothing to do with it."

I stopped speaking. During this last burst of speech, I had been talking faster and faster. Now I waited to hear what he would say.

Jack Tessa drummed his long, manicured fingers on the desk.

"They do not belong with their father."

I looked at him expectantly. He drummed his fingers some more.

"Okay. One, you need to get your ex-husband to give up his parental rights. I can draw up the papers. He has to sign them. You're safest with that. He would no longer have to pay you child support, but it sounds like that's not going to impact you much. What about after you're gone? Will the children need that money?"

"No."

"You're certain."

I nodded. "I have a large life insurance policy that, thank God, some insurance guy talked me into when I became a single parent. I have another policy through the newspaper. Not so big, but enough to set aside for their college. I have a 401K, social security. I almost own my house outright, thanks to my inheritance after my father died. The roof leaks and the bathrooms have 1970s avocado tile, but it's a solid home. They'll be okay, and Michael makes an excellent living."

"It's a tough one. You came here because I don't bull-shit anyone. Ex-spouses and families have a way of turning strange when death and money come into play. I've seen families with estates worth millions fight to the death over a single set of sterling silver tableware. I've seen the worst of people—and I rarely see the best. I don't ever see two sisters fighting over great-grandma's table linens and one sister just gives in rather than fight. I see people want to draw blood in court, and they come to me because they think I can do it. So you need to think about what your ex is capable of, and what he might really do when the chips are down. Think about it."

"I have thought about it. Look, Mr. Tessa, 'when the chips are down' is an expression. A cliché. But let me tell you, a person in my situation has to lay all her cards on the table. The chips *are* down. And it's a bad hand and I'm just trying to make the best of it. You'll draw up all these papers?"

He nodded. "But only you can talk your ex into signing."

"Leave that to me."

"Done."

He stood and shook my hand. It was cool and dry. Mine was sweaty.

He escorted me to the door. "I'll have my secretary call you when the papers are ready for you to pick up.

Think about what I've said. You're very smart, Ms. Waters. You'll do the right thing."

I shut the door. Out in my car, my knees started trembling and my teeth chattered. I had told Harry to let them pull the plug after two weeks. Fourteen days. And I needed David to sign papers giving our children to me so I could give them to someone else. Lawyers and death. What a pair.

20

Michael

My whole life has been a baseball analogy. When life gets me down, I say it's bottom of the ninth, two outs, bases loaded. I still have one more at bat. Sometimes life throws you a knuckleball. Sometimes a fastball.

In my life, the Big Pitcher Upstairs usually throws me a curveball, kind of low. So it was when I met George.

I have never been monogamous. I've had periods of my life where I was a total whore. It was the lifestyle of the time. It was Studio 54. Even when I settled down, when AIDS came along and killed half my friends, I just never went looking for a soul mate. Maybe Lily's right. What we have is so close to perfect, except for the sex part, that we both got kind of lazy about finding someone.

Maybe it's that, for most gay men, the whole settle down and get married thing didn't even start to be a blip on our radar until gay men could safely come out of the closet—the 1990s, maybe. And "safe" is relative. I live in New York. Forget some other places where I think hiding in the closet remains the only option if you value your safety. And it all depends on your family, too. Your world. You can't play pro sports and be gay. I don't even think you could be a sportswriter and gay. Fireman…pushing it. I mean, legally you can do some things and the courts would even back you. But at what price? My father hasn't spoken to me since I transferred to a different college after my assault. When it rains, I get an ache in my upper left thigh—where my femur was broken—that almost makes me want to go to bed. But that ache is nothing compared to what I lost when I was in that locker room and afterward.

Still, commitment ceremonies—those are new. And marriages—in Canada and Vermont. Also new. I would read about these changes on the landscape of America. I would also read how some people worried these changes were literally causing the demise of all that was good and right about America. Undermining marriage. Well, straight people have had a fifty percent divorce rate for some time without us gays coming into the picture.

However, despite the new options, the new possibilities, I can't say as I ever felt this longing for a soul mate—for the other "half" of me. I didn't feel less than whole without a spouse.

For Valentine's Day, Lily and I were dining at the latest hot spot on the Upper East Side. I made reservations a month in advance through Lily's paper's restaurant critic. Tara offered to babysit Noah because Justin was going to a family wedding so she was going to be alone and crabby on Valentine's Day anyway. Lily took a lot of Compazine so she wouldn't throw up the delicious meal for which I would be paying in the neighborhood of two hundred bucks (before tip), and donned the new red silk scarf I gave her on her now-bald head. She pinned a rhinestone butterfly to the front of her turban and looked vaguely like a gypsy fortune-teller. I admire her that she never bought a wig. It's bald or the scarf, but she isn't going to deal with a head of fake-looking hair, itchy no less. Actually, at the start of chemo, she did buy a wig. She opted for a white platinum punk wig that made her look like a hooker. Have to hand it to her. She says "Fuck you" to cancer just as well as she says "Fuck you" to me when she's mad.

We were sitting at a prime table at Giorgio's—three-and-a-half stars in the *Times*—and laughing our way through the night. Toward the end of the evening, around 11:00, the crowd was thinning a little bit—though not too much because it was Valentine's Day, after all. And out came the chef. He stopped at table after table. Not my type, really. A little bit chubby, dark hair (I like blondes). He was very charming, though, and knew food. And call it "gaydar," but I sensed he wasn't straight.

"You enjoy your meal?" he asked us. He had the tiniest hint of an Italian accent, and when he smiled he had a single dimple at the top of his left cheek. His eyes were dark brown, framed with the longest lashes I had ever seen. He looked at Lily's scarf, and he welled up. I think he thought we were lovers and here she was a tragic Valentine's Day figure on the most romantic night of the year. He got the tragedy part right, but not the rest.

"It was magnificent," Lily smiled. She was loopy. In addition to the Compazine she'd taken, she'd smoked some grass (courtesy of Ellie, whose new boyfriend grew it in his attic under heat lamps) and had drunk two glasses of wine.

"The sauce on my pasta was magnificent," I said.

"Thank you." He looked at me intently.

I didn't want him to leave our table. I fumbled for something to say. "I'm sure you hear all the time how people are amateur chefs, but I love food and love to cook and I can't tell you how impressed I was with the presentation, and with our waiter. Terrific service."

"You cook?" He turned to me.

I nodded. "I'm Italian, too. I make a mean spaghetti sauce." I know I wanted him to stay at our table, but I couldn't believe how banal and pathetic I sounded. *I'm Italian, too?* What was this? A Knights of Columbus meeting? "I can do French foods pretty well—"

"Very well." Lily slurred a little. She patted my arm. "My best friend here can outcook anyone. Even you, I bet." She pointed a finger at George and winked. In the candlelight, she looked ethereal. Fragile, yet glowing.

Suddenly George, the name stitched onto his chef

coat, cocked an eyebrow. "I would have guessed you two were married."

"My mother wishes," I said, "but I'm afraid we're both waiting for a knight in shining armor."

As soon as I said it, I wondered again what the fuck was wrong with me. I never out myself. Not that I'm ashamed of my sexuality, but I just don't make a habit of announcing it. And George wasn't my type at all. He was sweaty from being in the kitchen. And did I mention chubby? I've always been one of those gay men who demands bodily perfection from a lover—after all, I'm "perfect" myself. But something drew me to him.

He smiled. "Me, too."

At that, a sous chef motioned for him, poking her head out the kitchen door. He smiled at us, and did he hold my gaze a few seconds, or was I imagining things? I'd taken a hit or two of Lily's joint. Maybe it was all in my mind. Then again, doesn't everyone hit on me? "A crisis calls." George motioned toward the kitchen and shrugged. "Please, don't leave yet. Dessert is on me. And a brandy."

When he went back into the kitchen, Lily grabbed my hand, "You were flirting!"

"I was not."

"What's with the knight in shining armor shit? You never do that. Never. You *like* him."

"Don't."

"He is totally not your type."

"Exactly."

"Which is why he's perfect for you."

"What?" I pulled my hand away. "You better stop drinking."

"Don't you get it? You always pick the wrong guy for you. Here's a guy who cooks, who's into food. Listen to the music he has picked for his restaurant. You love Boccelli. He owns the place, so he's not a loser who's going to hit you up for money like Craig—ugh, he was a loser. No, this guy's the one."

"Lily, I'm really not in the market for a new boyfriend right now."

"Since when have you ever had a boyfriend? You have *boy-toys*. It's time to grow up. And he's perfect. We're staying. We're closing this place up. You are giving him your number. And if you don't do it, you know I will."

"Please. I know. You're such a yenta. But I don't have time for a relationship." I heard myself saying these things, and I also heard, as I know Lily did, that for the first time I didn't mean them.

We closed the place. We called Tara and told her not to wait up. We drank brandy. Lily got drunk. I got drunker.

Near the end of the night, George joined our table. He talked about how he studied in Italy and France. He talked about his food influences. He spoke about opera and art and growing up Italian. He was short; he was chubby. I was smitten.

At one point, Lily excused herself to the ladies' room.

"Your friend? She is very sick?"

I nodded. "She has cancer."

He shook his head. "She's very beautiful. Such a shame. Such a shame. And she has children. I hope she gets better."

"I think she might die." I stared down at my brandy, and a choked-off guttural sound escaped from me. Sort of a stifled sob. "What the fuck?" I said aloud. "I'm sorry. She just looks beautiful tonight, and we've had a great time. It's hard."

"She is lucky to have you."

"Thanks. I've known her twenty years almost."

"Listen…I—I hope you come here again."

"Look, if I don't give you my number, Lily will, so you might as well call me. She'll be impossible if we don't at least meet somewhere for a drink." I wrote my home number on my business card.

He smiled and mopped at his brow with a cloth napkin. He tucked the napkin into his apron when he was through.

"I'd like that. I work crazy hours, you know. The restaurant."

"I'm not looking to get married. Maybe I'm just looking for a friend."

Lily was practically squealing in the cab on the way to the train station.

"I want to know every detail. I am so jealous."

"Yeah, well…we haven't even done anything yet."

A week later, we had. We went to a movie—he liked foreign films with subtitles and old movies. Just like me. And he held my hand in the dark. I found my palms sweating like some high school kid on the night of his prom. We went back to his place, a beautiful apartment facing the East River. He had black-and-white photographs hanging on the walls, matted and framed. Venice and Florence. The Italian countryside. He must have spent a fortune to redo his kitchen, which was enormous by Manhattan standards. We made cream sauce for fresh raspberries and ate them at his dining room table.

"You might as well know," he said, "I'm intimidated as hell about being with you. I don't know that I've ever seen a more beautiful man."

"They all say that," I joked.

"And I might as well tell you it's been a while for me. I'm a workaholic."

"Well, I'm a slut. And you know, I can't explain why I feel so comfortable with you."

We made love. And like that, we were a couple. Albeit a couple with conflicting schedules and conflicting lives. I felt guilty, too, for finding love when Lily needed me most, but George never pushed. He was a workaholic, and maybe it never would have worked if I hadn't been so busy with Lily. Maybe what I thought was a curveball was actually straight across the middle of home plate.

"Hey George," I said one night, across a tray of lasagna I'd cooked for him. I'd gained six pounds since we started dating. He'd gained three.

"Yeah?"

"I forgot the most important question of all."

"Yes, Michael?"

"Yankees or Mets?"

"How can you even ask? Could I hold my head up on the streets of New York if I was anything but a Yankees fan?"

It was love. A home run.

21

Unholy House
by Lily Waters

I lived in a godless house.

On Sunday, while my playmates leaned scraped knees on church kneelers, wriggling and sliding on shiny wooden pews under the annoyed gazes of their mothers, I learned how to pull a dollar bill from under a shot glass without spilling a drop. The next day, I brought a shot glass and a dollar in for Show and Tell, much to the chagrin of my second-grade teacher. I learned from her shocked gaze and the awed stares of my classmates that visiting bars in the less fashionable neighborhoods of New York City on Sundays was considered unholy.

When I hear my girlfriends recount their childhoods, they complain about distant fathers and overbearing mothers. Lisa tells me about the year she nearly made the Olympic swim team—only to have her accomplishments overshadowed by her brother's Hail Mary pass in the final game of the season, which lifted his team to the state championships—and exalted him to a football scholarship. Her father went to every football game. He never made it to a swim meet. Others tell of adolescent screaming matches and sneaking out past curfew. Alcoholism, sexual abuse, a sister confined to a psychiatric hospital. I listen to my friends' stories, and when it comes time to hear about my Sundays and my house, they regard *me* with pity. As if somehow a dimly lit bar and a pack of tough guys slamming their money down is no place for a little girl. But I learned more from Big Jimmy and John the bartender and the colorful crew with their nicknames out of a Scorsese film—Trigger, Snake Eyes, Larry the Lip—than I would have learned in any catechism class.

Certainly, I learned persistence. The sole purpose of the Shot Glass Shuffle, after all, was to free my dad to have a few beers while I struggled to learn my trick. I sat for hours patiently learning under the tutelage of the Barroom King.

But bar tricks aside, I learned all the Judeo-Christian values preached about on Sabbaths everywhere. I watched my dad's rough crowd take care of skid row bums who came in from the cold to get warm and beg for a beer. My father and Uncle Jim talked to these trembling, toothless men as equals, making sure they got a sandwich and didn't go hungry that night. Theirs was a no-holier-than-thou approach. They didn't belittle the life these men led as wrong or sinful. Those ragged and filthy Bowery bums were hard-luck cases. One wrong turn, one jail stint turned ugly, and it could have been any one of them sitting on the stool, trying to escape the cold.

I also learned what true brotherhood meant. My dad always told me if anything happened to him, my uncle Jim, no blood relative but a blood brother of the streets, would take care of me. I never pinned my hopes on ethereal guardian angels, but instead on iron workers and construction foremen, on the occasional ex-con and on bartenders. These men would shelter me from harm. They would kill for me. My father traveled the city streets with a switchblade in his pocket and a crowbar under the seat of his car. He told me I had to be willing to kill for my family because that is the way things are in Yorkville and on mean streets. I learned Darwin's survival of the fittest from a master.

No preacher or priest would stand in the pulpit and praise the blade and the bar. That type of justice was not preached at the Sermon on the Mount. But the bond, unable to be broken, remains. My father "made it." He pulled himself up from the streets to marry a nice girl and raise a daughter in the suburbs. He got a college degree at night and took a union job. He paid his dues. He followed the rules. But even as he "got respectable," he never forgot where he came from.

I never much thought about why we never went to church, except when my mother's parents came to visit. Polish-Catholics, boisterous and loving, her family revered the Pope and made certain we knew The Lord's Prayer and the Ten Commandments.

But once Grandma and Pop returned home after a visit, the prayers stopped. We never even went to church once a year on Easter. Never attended a Midnight Mass. My father taught me that hypocrisy is the lowliest form of cowardice. I learned that if I claimed to believe in something, I had to be able to defend it. I could not throw my name behind a concept or word like "Christian" or "feminist" as a matter of convenience. I cannot hide behind the shield of a word or phrase, I must *be* the embodiment of what I believe.

When I turned fifteen, I finally found out my father didn't believe in God at all. He was not a fence-sitter playing both sides "just in case." Not an agnostic, he was an atheist. If there is a God, he used to say, why are children abused? Why is there war? At fifteen, I didn't have a good answer for him. But Dad taught me to think for myself. He brought up the big questions of the ages. He challenged me to find the answers.

I became a woman unafraid to ask for what she wants, gutsy when she needs to be. There is something to be said for standing your ground, even if it means a fight. I don't want people in my life who can't say what they think. I cringe when I see people talk down to children. Eye to eye, face-to-face, let them know truth.

After years of Sundays in bars where cigar smoke clung to the paneling and swirled around slow-turning ceiling fans, I discovered the life lessons my friends from religious households did. I learned about loving your brother. About tolerance and respect. About honoring family. And I still acquired something akin to faith.

The concept of our aloneness in the universe terrifies us. The passage to an unknown at the moment of death is rarely even spoken about. Our fragility as humans is denied. We bury our corpses with waxenlike makeup in an effort to preserve a sense of life about them even in death. But God's house is not a church. It can be a bar. It can be a soup kitchen. Perhaps she is everywhere. Perhaps he is a Barroom King. If a messiah can be born in a manger, God can live in smoky bar.

I only see now what a unique universe I grew up in. Then, as I clutched my shot glass and brought it to class, I thought mine was a childhood like all others. I thought my classmates learned about five-card stud and pitching pennies against a dirty curb. But it was my world. And it made me what I am today. A woman striving to avoid hypocrisy. Atheists are unique in this world of stargazers and prayer-sayers. My childhood world was one of foamy beers in highball glasses sitting on a barstool, high above the floor, unable to get down. Watching the weary travel in and out the doors. Learning the Shot Glass Shuffle.

Then, at the end of the day spent with Dad, I'd come home to the embrace of my mother, who believed the world could be viewed through, not just rose-colored glasses, but fuchsia ones. I had a dichotomy there. Now, both my parents are gone, so is the old bar, the friends of my father's who dwelt

there. I can't hear them, but sometimes, sometimes
I can smell them, in a bar, the scent of yeast. And
I suppose, for me, it's as close to heaven as I may get.

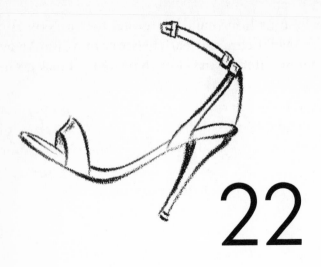

22

Lily

How can you possibly cram a lifetime of lessons, everything you want your kids to know, into months, days or even a couple of years?

Justin, Tara's boyfriend, is pretty much everything you'd want in your daughter's first boyfriend. He is polite. He shakes Michael's hand when he comes over. He gives me a hug now, as we've all grown closer. He wears a single little earring, a tiny gold hoop that if my high school boyfriend wore, my father would have beaten him up on the front lawn. Of course, no one ever said my dad was a very good parent, so I think the earring is just fine. A nose ring might have given me a jolt, but Justin is an A student, bound for college, and he wants to be a physical therapist and specialize in sports medicine. His dream job would be to work for the New York Yankees. Michael would let Tara marry him. Tomorrow. If Justin eventually gets a job with the New York Yankees, Michael will kick in a sizable dowry.

When I first lost my hair, Justin even got a supershort buzz cut as a show of solidarity. If Justin has a flaw, it is that he is cute. Too cute. If I was young and my hormones were going crazy, he would be the type of guy I would have sex. I worry about this.

"Sweetie?" I said to Tara one Sunday as we watched *Guys and Dolls* together for possibly the thousandth time. We were curled on my bed with a big bowl of popcorn, an afghan thrown over my knees. She was drinking a diet soda and twirling a tendril of hair as we both sighed over Marlon Brando. Singing. Michael considers this a mortal sin. Brando should not sing. Was not meant to sing. He was meant to wear a ripped T-shirt in *A Streetcar Named Desire*. But Tara and I forgive Marlon.

"Yeah, Mom?"

"I think Justin is a really terrific guy."

Teens have a bullshit meter fine-tuned from miles away.

"And?" she asked warily.

"I was just wondering…if you two were thinking about having sex. If maybe," I said hurriedly, "you wanted to talk to me about anything."

She sat bolt upright in my bed.

"What's that supposed to mean?"

As the young, very sexy Marlon Brando sang "Luck Be a Lady Tonight," I felt decidedly unlucky. Why did I bring it up?

"It's just that I want you to know that if you ever need to talk to me about anything, I'm here. I think he's terrific, but I also want you to be careful."

Tara's eyes registered fury. "You are so damn transparent, Mom. You invite me in here for some mother/ daughter time, and it's all just bullshit—"

"Tara!"

"It is! No, I am not sleeping with Justin. We haven't even talked about it. Okay…maybe we have, but we're not going to do anything stupid."

I started crying. It wasn't fair, crying. It's a cheap shot if used as a weapon, and I hadn't intended to. I couldn't help it.

"It's just that in all the cancer books they talk about kids acting out. Kids of parents who are sick or siblings of cancer patients. I just don't want what's happening to me to make you feel as if I am too sick to pay attention to you. So that you have to go elsewhere."

Every parent recalls the precise moment when they first shifted roles with their children. For me it was the time my father came over. Years ago. And he looked old. For the first time, I saw the lines of hard living, and I realized he was "old." For Tara and me, this was our moment. She leaned over and hugged me. Then she kissed me on the forehead—I mean, who was the child here?—and whispered, "It's okay, Mom. I don't feel like that."

I sniffled. "Thanks."

She stroked my barely-there hair. "I love you, Mom. Sorry I got all bent out of shape."

I shrugged. "You know, as long as we're getting some stuff out in the open, I really need to ask you something."

"What?"

I paused, then plunged ahead. "If I died, I mean, not from cancer, but say I got hit by a bus, do you want to go to England with your father, or would you prefer to live here with Michael?"

"You're not going to die, Mom. You can't."

"Well, I really should have dealt with this a long time ago. So let's say this is purely hypothetical, which is it?"

"I'm not going to England."

"So it's Michael."

"No, it's you." She stared at me stubbornly.

"Think long and hard about this. Sometimes you and Michael bicker."

"I have."

"I'm going to fly over to London to talk to your father."

"Does he know you're coming?"

"Not yet. But I've thought about it. This isn't about him and me. This is about you and Noah. Michael is the closest thing you have to a real father. And Ellie as a guardian—"

"Let's not go there…" Tara shuddered dramatically, overemphasizing a look of horror on her face. We both laughed.

"England could be a wonderful experience…living overseas."

"I don't want to live there. If you go see my dad, can I come to London, too?"

I looked at her. What if she came to London with me and loved it? Wanted to become a London punk rocker, or go to Oxford? Where would that leave Noah?

"Sure. You miss your dad?"

"No. God, Mom, you think I don't recognize your handwriting?"

"Huh?"

"All the years you bought Christmas presents and birthday presents, and signed the card 'Love, Dad.' Did you think that just by writing it with your left hand, or getting Uncle Michael to forge Dad's signature, that I wouldn't figure it out? For God's sake, Mom, Noah's onto the whole charade. I'm more curious than anything. And I suppose if I have to decide something big like this, I want to see if he misses me."

"Of course he does."

"Did you know his wife has never actually spoken to me on the telephone? We have to call him at the university. And you know, I just stopped calling after a while. *Months* would go by without hearing from him, Mom. *Months.* He always blamed it on the time difference. As if people in England and New York couldn't possibly figure out a way to connect."

"I know."

"Hey, Mom? What's so great about her that he'd dump us all?"

I bit my tongue. *She's got a set of knock-out tits and had the sex drive of a typical college student when he met her, not the sex drive of a woman in her thirties throwing up every two hours in the throes of a difficult pregnancy. Oh, and her par-*

ents are immensely wealthy, and at the time, we were lucky we had enough money for diapers, let alone the new washing machine we needed. Tara didn't need to know all that. She was bright. She'd figure it out.

The next day, I told Michael I was going to Europe. He was over, cooking supper. George was working. They were great together, and I was thrilled for Michael.

"You shouldn't be flying. Planes are just airborne germ factories."

"I don't have a choice."

"You do. Can't you handle this all by phone? Can't lawyers handle it?"

"No."

"I mean, this is the guy who dumped you. You need 'face time,' as Joe would say? After all this time?"

"Michael, you and I have been 'tabling' this whole guardian decision for four months now. I am asking him to give up his parental rights. I have papers for him to sign. I want you to be their guardian."

"Think you might have wanted to confirm that with me before you took off on Virgin Atlantic? It's too much responsibility."

"I know you're going to agree with me sooner or later."

"Do you think I don't love them?"

"No. I never said that."

"This is all wrenching, Lily. It's like I have two lives. One is normal. And one is full of death and horrible decisions. And my so-called normal existence is as a gay man. So what does that say to you?"

"What? You're a homosexual?"

He rolled his eyes.

"I can't believe after all these years I find out you're gay. I'm shocked. Dismayed. Disgusted."

"Please, Lily, be serious."

"I'm seriously going to London."

"Fine. Go."

He continued stirring the marinara sauce, furiously. I saw his eyes move from the pot of sauce, to the refrigerator. Magnets with silly sayings like "My Mom Can't Cook. Open Refrigerator with Caution," and "Greetings from Florida" from a trip down South, held up "priceless" art from Noah and Tara. Report cards vied with postcards, which vied with snapshots from Halloween and Christmas, and even a footprint from when Noah was born stamped to a white piece of paper.

"Be careful," Michael said more softly. "Don't catch anything. Could be dangerous with your white blood count so low."

"I know."

"I need time to think this through."

"I know."

He kept stirring. "At least if I had them they'd eat well."

I laughed. "And know the Yankee lineup."

"Those things are important."

"Exactly."

I stood in back of him on my tiptoes and kissed the back of his neck. I slipped my arms around his waist. Then I pinched his ass. "For a gay guy, you're pretty hot. I bet you could bounce a quarter on that ass."

"You're exasperating."

"That's why you love me."

"I suppose," he said softly, "you're right."

That night we ate dinner together. Later, when the house was quiet, I logged onto my computer and looked at flights. What do you say to the man who took your heart and sent it through a Cuisinart?

"I have to work late. I think I'll just crash on the couch in my office, okay, baby?"

"No, it's not okay, David. This is the second time this week. I'm eight months pregnant—that would be GI-NORMOUS in layman's terms. Huge! And I'm running after Tara. And what if I go into labor in the middle of the night?"

"You have four weeks to go. You're not going into labor."

"I hate when you do that."

"Do what?" His voice was edgy, weary-sounding.

"Act like you know what's going to happen and what's good for me. Michael brings me a pint of heavenly hash ice cream when I'm tired and exhausted. *You* suggest going for a walk so I don't gain too much weight. As if the weight is more important than making me feel a little better, if only for a half hour."

"Yeah. But then Michael isn't going to have to hear you bitching that none of your jeans fit after this baby is born. Look…you're not going to go into labor."

"Are you cheating on me?" The question hung in the air. Like a lot of things. All our conversations were now punctuated with venomous words like "always," as in "*You* always…," or "never." I wasn't really sure what had happened, but I assumed that me getting up to pee eleven times a night had something to do with me being testy, and his not getting sex as often as he used to had something to do with *his* getting testy. But lately, he had stopped pressing for it altogether.

"You're insane, you know that? Clinically insane. Maybe you should see a shrink."

"I'm sorry."

"You should be."

He hung up the phone on me, and I sat in my bedroom and sobbed. I went to the bathroom and got an entire *roll* of toilet paper. A roll! And I sat there and made my way through it, blowing my nose and dabbing at my eyes. How could I accuse him of such a horrendous thing? After all, I had been difficult to live with lately, and he was working so hard to get his second anthology together.

He couldn't be having an affair. We were going to have another baby, for God's sake. A sign of how much we loved each other.

Prick is not a strong enough word for David. Well, Michael and I seriously considered calling him Prick. But we decided, when Noah was little, that him overhearing the word prick wasn't such a good idea. He could repeat it. Like to his preschool teacher at the time.

So we settled on Spawn of Satan—Spawn for short, the way we affectionately preferred to term him.

Our dear Spawn. And Child Bride. Occasionally just The Bride.

He deserved his moniker.

He had hung up on me.

He had suggested that I see a shrink.

I took a deep breath.

I wondered if, when—if?—I got to heaven, God would let me put a hex on Spawn. Or do angels play nice all the time?

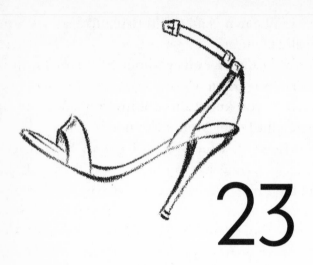

23

Michael

Out of the clear blue sky, some guy named Pete called Lily for a date. He contacted her voice mail at the paper. She was still managing to eke out her column every week, and Joe would assign her some features during weeks she felt good. Chemo was over, and she was doing radiation.

I'm Noah's baseball coach, and spring training had started. He was in the shower, and I was boiling water for some pasta. She came home from the office—one of her face-time days with Joe—and said, "I have a date to-night." She said it as if she were shocked.

"A date?"

She nodded. "With a guy who apparently doesn't mind dating a woman with a crew cut." Her hair had started growing in just the tiniest bit. Her eyebrows were still drawn on.

"You're beautiful even without hair. Don't you remember when Demi Moore did it for *G.I. Jane?*"

"Michael, you know, I'm not insecure about my appearance. But Demi Moore I'm not."

"It's a look."

"Yeah. It's a cancer look."

"Well, obviously, whoever this guy is, he's a man of substance and sees past the fact your right eyebrow is drawn on crooked and down into your inner soul and inner bitchiness. And apparently, he feels he can put up with that. Deluded man. Who is he?"

"Pete Bartlett."

"Who's he…wait, is he that math teacher from your chemo encounter?"

"Yes. He has hair now. He's in remission. He had the good cancer."

"Good cancer." Michael snorted.

"He did. Hodgkins."

"Well…look at this turn of events. Lily with a date."

"You act like this is something surprising."

"Hmm…call it a hunch, but I haven't seen that particular sparkle in your eye since you met Spawn. Of course, here's hoping this one is a keeper. A real keeper."

She was standing in her apartment wearing her most expensive high heels, her favorite lipstick and her best black cocktail dress, back when we lived down the hall from each other. A raging New Year's party was going on in her apartment, spilling out into the hall in the way New York City parties do—the apartments are just too small. It was wall-to-wall revelers, and somewhere in the overheated, cramped living room was her brand-new fiancé.

"David asked me to marry him," she beamed, holding out her hand for me to admire the sparkling pear-shaped diamond perched on it.

"It's beautiful, Lily," I said without much enthusiasm, though the ring was pretty enough.

"Oh," she pouted, "don't be that way."

"Don't be what way?"

"That way. Try to act like you're actually happy for me."

"I am."

She pulled her hand back and turned around so I couldn't see her face.

"I *am* happy," I protested.

"No, you're not. You don't like David."

"All I ever said was I thought he was a bit of a rogue, so be careful. But I see you two are good together…." She still didn't turn around. "Maybe I'm just jealous."

"Jealous?" She turned around. "But you're *gay*. You're not even bi. We did that sloppy make-out session one night, but that was it."

"You know, *it's all about the sex* with you, isn't it?"

She howled. "Me? My God, you go through more guys in a week than I do in a year!"

"No need to get catty. I'm just saying that the only reason to be jealous isn't necessarily *S-E-X*."

"Well then, what?"

"Did you ever stop to think of the end of disco?"

Lily turned to the counter and poured herself a glass of champagne from the open bottle on the counter.

"I need this," she said. "I can tell you're going to be obtuse instead of direct. I'm ready now. Shoot."

"God, disco is dead."

"Tell that to those people in there." Though New Wave had taken over the airwaves, and we both loved The Clash, every time a disco song came on at a party, people still went wild.

I glanced through the door and could see friends dancing and singing out loud at the top of their lungs to "I Will Survive." "Yes, that's because half of your guests are gay. Nonetheless disco is dead. Studio 54 is gone. The Palladium is no longer the hot place to be. Cocaine isn't in every bathroom stall anymore. And you threw out your leg warmers."

"And that has to do with my getting engaged how?"

"It's just that I thought the party would never end. I thought you and I would live this crazy life, both of us writing, partying hard, dancing, dating, staying up all night, going to Greenwich Village...doing all the cool stuff we do. I thought we would keep doing it forever."

"Forever is a long time, Michael."

"Well, the party didn't have to be over so soon. Who am I going to play with now?"

"Considering I saw you sneak down the hall to your

apartment with two different guys tonight, I would say you probably won't ever hurt for playmates."

"But you know our *Moonlighting* nights. The nights when we pig out on pizza. Our shopping expeditions to the flea market—not to mention the Macy's day-after-Thanksgiving sale. It's the fucking Holy Grail of shopping. Now I won't have anyone to do that with."

"I'm getting married, I'm not entering the convent."

"Don't patronize me. Things have already changed some and they'll change more. And that's just life. I hate being a grown-up. I don't like change. And furthermore, can't a guy be a little jealous?"

She threw her arms around me neck and pecked my cheek. "I could always try to convert you to the other team."

"Not likely. But thanks."

A slow song came on—I think it was Lionel Ritchie of all things. Lily and I started slow dancing, and midway through the song, David came in. He gave us a strange look, and I stepped away from her. I stuck out my hand, "Congratulations, David."

"Thanks. I was just looking for my new fiancée." He tilted her chin up in a way I suppose he thought was sweet and endearing, and kissed her on the nose. I wanted to retch.

So ten months later, I was a groomsman in a black tux in their wedding. And I tried to make peace with the oh-so-smug-and-handsome Professor Waters. But in the end, he turned out to be the Spawn, and I was still here.

★ ★ ★

"So, is sex a possibility?" I asked as she tried to decide what to wear.

She paused and looked at me. "Hmm. I would say it's a definite maybe. Not in ordinary circumstances, but this guy…I mean, he just is different, Michael. He had left a voice-mail message once before, and I kind of blew it off. But he caught me off guard today and he had a million arguments why my being sick didn't matter. In fact, he numbered them like Letterman's Top Ten list."

"Clever."

"Number one was 'Cancer makes you skip through the bullshit.'"

"That it does."

"Agreed. So sex is a strong possibility. I mean, what would I be holding out for?"

She finally decided on a Donna Karan black bodysuit, a black wrap skirt, stiletto boots and a really pretty purple scarf around her head. She wore dangling earrings. Through this whole cancer ordeal, she had always made a point of wearing her lipstick, her heels, her best earrings. She did her makeup in a way to emphasize her lips, and she added a rhinestone pin to her scarf. She said it was akin to a mother's adage to always wear clean underwear—should she have to go to the hospital suddenly, at least she'd look damn good—the better to snag a handsome doctor.

She left to meet Pete at a restaurant, and I went to check on dinner. Then I took the stairs two at a time to Noah's room and knocked gently on the door. "It's me, Noah."

"Come in," he grumpily replied.

"Why the long face, kid?" I asked. He was lying on his bed, tossing a baseball into the air with his left hand and catching it in the mitt in his right. His hair was wet and tousled from his shower, and the damp towel was in a crumpled heap in the corner.

He shrugged. "I dunno."

I looked around his room. He had one foot still in real babyhood and one foot into he-man boyhood. On the shelf above his bed were stuffed animals of Elmo, Big Bird and Ernie, his favorite *Sesame Street* characters. I guessed he hadn't watched the show in a couple of years, but that shelf was his place of honor. Next to them was a picture of his mom and me. A framed school picture of his sister was on his dresser—she didn't make "the shelf." Next to the picture of Lily and me, taken when she was healthy and we were at the beach, was a ball I'd caught at a Yankees game before Noah was even born and signed by Don Mattingly. I'd given it to him for getting all A's on his last report card. And finally, on that shelf, was a Hot Wheels car in the shape of an Oscar Mayer Weiner. He found the car hysterically funny and "cool." It made the shelf.

Posters of the Yankees fought for wall space with artwork from school and colored pencil drawings he had done of cartoon characters. His pet goldfish, Reggie, named after Reggie Jackson, swam in a small aquarium amidst plastic seaweed.

Noah tossed the baseball in the air.

Toss. Catch.

"If something happens to Mom, who would take care of me?"

Toss. Catch.

"Well…" Toss. Catch. "If something did happen to her that she couldn't take care of you, then I would be here, of course. And I'd still take you to all the Yankees games." Toss. Catch.

"I'd rather live with you than anyone." Toss. Catch. Thud. He dropped the ball to the floor, and it rolled toward my feet.

"Well, you know, we'll see about that."

He stared at me, his eyes moist. I picked up the ball and gently tossed it to him. He caught it and resumed his game, staring at the ceiling and getting into a rhythm. Catch. Toss. Catch.

"You know, Noah, I can't say for sure what's going to happen. I just know that whatever does, we're still going to be best friends, just like we are now."

"Sure." His voice was hollow and flat.

I felt myself willing him to stop tossing the ball. Willing him to stop and cry and maybe get it out, all this shit no child should have to be dealing with. I walked closer to his bed so he'd have to see me out of the corner of his eye. When he tossed the ball, I grabbed it.

He glared at me. "Why should I believe you? Mom said she would be fine, but she's not. I can tell the way she's tired all the time. Nothing anyone says is true. *You* told me she would be fine." It was an indictment in the court of a little boy.

"We didn't lie to you. The cancer lied to us."

"It doesn't matter. And if something happens to Mom…" He looked at the wall.

I sat down on the bed, and cupped his chin in my hand, turning his head toward me. "If something happens to Mom, what?"

"Then what? I can't go to my *real* father. He doesn't even know me. I bet you if he walked into my school right now, he wouldn't be able to tell which kid was his. You're my dad. I tell the kids at soccer and baseball and everything that you're…my dad. I don't really say it, but if they think you're my dad, I just don't tell them it's not true. And I don't want anything to change. You and Mom. And when you make me say my prayers, that's what I ask God for."

I didn't dare breathe. There it was.

"But you know your Mom and I are just friends, right?" I whispered.

"Yeah."

"And you know why, right?"

"Yeah. But it shouldn't matter."

I stifled a smile. Ah, if only I wasn't gay. It was like talking to a junior version of my mother.

"All I can promise is to not lie to you and to do my best to make sure nothing changes, that I'm always here."

I leaned over and hugged him. He stiffened and then I felt his shoulders tremble. I let him cry but didn't say anything else. It seemed like a "real man" thing to do. Noah and I always joked about that. Real men don't eat quiche. Yeah right. I love quiche. But real men don't like the Mets. They don't put ketchup on hot dogs, and they don't forget to say their prayers. Real men are complex that way.

I let go of him and stood up. "Brace yourself. I saw your mother bought some kind of fake egg mix for breakfast tomorrow."

"Barf."

"Agreed."

I went downstairs. The thought that Noah and Tara—as self-centered and difficult as she was now, at sixteen, not to mention her abysmal attempts at learning to drive—would end up with Spawn bothered me. I thought back to the night of David and Lily's engagement. I thought the party would go on forever. But we all have to grow up sometime.

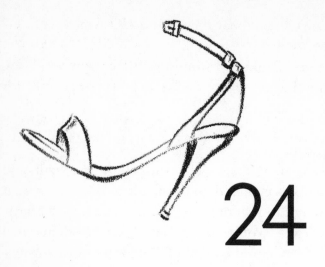

24

Curveball
An excerpt from a novel by Michael Angelo

Sam spent his life perfecting his batting stance. He learned to stare down the pitcher, to bend his knees, to raise his bat, ready. To have every nerve and muscle on alert, waiting for whatever pitch was sent his way, in life or in the ballgame. He lived and breathed baseball, the smell of a leather glove, the sound of the ball smacking against the bat, the sight of its high arc as it shot out of the park.

Sam knew that since baseball's beginnings, sportswriters have used the game as a metaphor for life. Men who couldn't talk to their fathers about anything important, about anything emotional, men who could do little more than punch their dad in the arm, and mumble a few gruff words, found in baseball a way to communicate.

Sam and his father used baseball to talk before Sam went off to college. They would play catch in the backyard. On the face of it, catch is such a simple game. Sam loved the rhythm. He threw the ball to his father. His father threw it back. Sam loved the sound of the ball hitting the leather of his glove. His hand would wrap around it, and he would lob it back. If only, Sam used to think, their father-son relationship could be so simple. "Talk," in their case, was half phrases. "Good catch." "Nice throw." "Good arm."

Men of a certain generation could barely spit out the words, "I love you, son." Hugging was uncomfortable; kissing was out of the question. The ball, the glove, the game, the nosebleed seats at Shea Stadium or Fenway Park, or wherever the home team was playing, they were the pitcher's mound of communication. From there, the wind-up, and then the pitch over the plate in the form of verbal shorthand. *Dad really loved me,* men of that generation say, *he just didn't know how to show it.* But there's always the memories of Yankees games and hot dogs, and the ritual of buying a bag of peanuts and letting the shells fall to the cement and hearing them crunch under your sneakers.

Sam told himself the words "nice catch" were just a secret father-son code for the real stuff. Then he was assaulted.

First the police came. He drifted in and out of a morphine haze. The detectives—two of them—kept asking him, like they didn't believe him.

"Son...now you're sayin' you didn't see nothin' of the fellas that did this to you?"

Sam's doctor told the detectives it might be shock. Or the trauma. "He could even have amnesia of the trauma event. It's not uncommon. Let him recover a bit and perhaps it will come back to him."

No one from the team visited.

His coach didn't drop by.

In fact, not a single person from his college—the people he'd been friends with through thick and thin—none of them even came to see if Sam was going to live.

His mother flew in with his father. She never left his side. Night and day she said prayers, or she pushed the hair off of his forehead and cooed to him. She whispered in his ear, "You will get well, Sam. You will get well."

His father didn't come by the hospital but for the first day. Then, when Sam slowly started emerging from the morphine haze, his mother felt safe enough to leave him one morning and to go back to her hotel and shower and rest. It was then his father arrived.

He stood at the foot of Sam's bed, surveying the mess of bruises, mottled and black. He looked at the catheter tube that snaked its way into Sam's penis.

"I hear they found a black plastic dick at the scene."

He said it. Left that sentence hanging in the air. It was the one screw-up the coach and team had made. The one thing they should have taken but didn't.

"Don't remember," Sam croaked out.

"I smell something sick. Something rotten. I

talked to your best friend, Charlie. Or should I say ex-best friend?"

Sam opened his eyes a crack. The monitors beeped, and he was sure because his heart was pounding hard. He felt his mouth go drier than it already was.

"I know why they did this to you. When you get out of here, you come on home, you get your things and you tell your poor mama that you're moving away. And if you come back to visit, you make sure you do it when I'm not there."

His father turned his back and walked toward the door. Sam felt tears on his cheeks. He couldn't move his hand to wipe them away.

"If it was me that was your coach, I would have done no different."

And those were the last words Sam's father ever spoke to him.

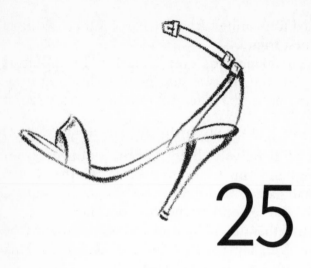

25

Lily

Pete told me I looked beautiful. He brought me a bunch of lilies of the valley—apparently the day we met I had mentioned something about how beautiful I thought they were. That having cancer makes you want to be around your favorite things and makes you want to not waste a second with the things you hate, including the people who bring you down.

We picked up where we left off, and by the end of the appetizer course, I knew I would make love with him. He made me dizzy, that's how crazy I was about him.

After dinner, we stood in the parking lot near our respective cars.

"You look great with hair, you know." I smiled.

"You've got some coming in, too."

"Pete…something about you…" I leaned in close to him and we kissed.

"Will you think I'm pushing it if I ask you back to my place for coffee?"

I shook my head.

I followed him to his apartment, which was two towns over—about a fifteen-minute ride. It was a duplex, a small house divided into an upstairs apartment and a downstairs apartment. His was downstairs, and he opened the door and ushered me inside.

Pete's apartment fit him. He had a fish tank with a few goldfish, and an old tabby cat named Chester that had once belonged to a student of his whose new baby brother turned out to be allergic.

His furniture wasn't "classic bachelor," but nice, comfy. I sat down on the couch while he went into the kitchen.

"Coffee or a nightcap? Or both? I have some sambuca."

"Sambuca would be great."

He returned with two snifters. "A woman after my heart. I love sambuca after a meal."

He set the snifters down on his coffee table, which had several books on space and astronomy. Then he sat next to me and next thing I knew we were kissing.

It had been so long since someone loved me in that way. And not just someone. It was Pete, who I felt understood me so innately. Even without this cancer connection, he was funny and really open and sincere. He was someone I was sure I could introduce my children to—something I rigorously avoided with ninety-nine percent of the men I'd ever dated since their father left.

"Stay a while?" he whispered.

I nodded, and he took my hand and led me to the bedroom. I slipped out of my skirt and boots. That left the bodysuit. I slid the straps down. Then I reached back and undid my bra.

As I slid my bra and bodysuit down, I had a moment, a flash, of worry. The scar from where they'd removed my lump was still raw and red—and radiation hadn't helped it any. My skin there looked like a bad sunburn. Peeling.

Pete, by now, was in this adorable pair of scotch plaid boxers. Flannel. He was to me in three strides, and the first thing he did was lower his lips to my poor wounded right breast. He kissed the nipple, and then the scar. He kissed the scar again and moved his tongue over it. Then he went to my other breast, as if to signify they weren't different from each other. Then he stood and looked me in the eyes and said, "You have a beautiful body." He put his hands to the knot on my scarf and undid it. The purple silk fluttered to the floor.

"And you have a beautiful face," he whispered.

I felt my eyes tearing up, and I just pressed against him, kissing him hard. We made our way to the bed, and it was one of those lovemaking experiences that you replay over and over again. Not because the orgasm was so much better or his cock was so much bigger. But because it was so intensely honest.

Afterward, I lay there for an hour or so, cradled in his arms, before I said, "I have to go home."

"I know. Call me when you get there, to say good-night? I won't go to sleep until I know you made it home safe."

I nodded and slid from out of his bed. He had flannel sheets—soft and warm. Guess he was a flannel fan. He also got out of bed and pulled on sweatpants and a sweatshirt. Then, after I was dressed, he walked me out to my car and kissed me again in the dark.

"I had such a good time, Lily. Can I see you again? Like tomorrow?"

I laughed. "My kids…you know…they take up a lot of my time. But yes, we'll work something out."

"I'm so glad you agreed to go out with me. I worked on that Top Ten list for a month. I even ran it by my Cancer Survivors Group."

"Well, you can tell them it worked."

I climbed in my car and drove home. Michael's car wasn't there. I let myself in, let Gunther out and went up to check on Noah. He was sleeping peacefully, looking angelic. I picked up a damp towel and his dirty clothes, and walked to the end of the hall where I keep the laundry basket. I could see Tara's light on. I pressed my ear to the door. Her stereo was on quiet. I knocked gently. "I'm home. You up?"

"Yeah."

I opened the door and poked my head in. Her bed was covered with homework.

"Tara! It's 1:00 a.m."

"I know. I have a chemistry test tomorrow. I'm going to sleep now, I swear."

"You'll end up sick, not sleeping enough."

"Yes, Oh Nagging One."

"Thanks. Now shut off the light."

"How was your date?"

"Who told you I was on a date?"

"Uncle Michael. How was it?"

"Really nice."

"Awesome, Mom. You know, Uncle Michael's great, but…it would be nice if you had a real boyfriend. People will think you're a fag hag."

"What!"

"Chill out, Mom. God, you act like I don't know anything."

I shook my head and shut her door, then went down to my bedroom. I dialed Pete's number.

"Night-night, Pete."

"Good night, gorgeous."

"A woman could get used to compliments like that."

"A man could get used to having a beautiful woman like you to sleep next to."

"I better get some sleep."

"'Night. I'll call you tomorrow."

"Good night," I whispered.

Okay, so I had chemo to thank for the best sex of my life. Maybe for the love of my life.

They say hell hath no fury like a woman scorned. But hell ain't seen nothin' like a woman out to protect her children.

Pete and I were seeing each other fast and furiously,

and Michael was head over heels in love with George. And two weeks later, I flew to London with Tara.

I met David for dinner at my hotel. Tara was seeing a play with a tour group, pleased to be free of her mother for the night and probably passing herself off as eighteen to the handsome young tour guide with the slight Irish brogue. I wanted the advantage of being seated in the restaurant first, so I got a table for two and waited for David to show up.

I hadn't seen him in five years, and I hoped he had lost his hair, grown a gut and had the disheveled appearance of a man aimless without his first wife. When he entered the restaurant, I saw none of those things. His hair was still thick and sandy blond. Maybe he was graying, but you couldn't tell from across the room. He didn't have a gut, just the taut, lean lines I remembered. He wasn't frumpy or wrinkled, but dressed in a crisp white Oxford shirt, gray slacks and expensive black loafers.

He walked confidently across the dining room, the walk of someone who always knows he is the best-looking man at a party. At one time, that walk, knowing he was cutting across the room to me, would make my stomach do flip-flops. Now, I felt nothing but a dull anger I thought I had long since spent to nothingness. I'd take Pete's swaggerless walk any day.

I didn't stand to greet him. I think he expected a hug, and he leaned down awkwardly to kiss me, his eyes glancing around the room as if to see if anyone had noticed my slight snubbing of him.

"Lily…" His lips brushed my cheek. He smelled of Polo.

"David." I didn't smile as he sat down.

His gray eyes looked at my scarf, at my face, at the toll cancer had taken on my coloring. My makeup was perfect, but still, I knew I looked very different from the last time he'd seen me. I saw the muscle of his jaw flex several times. His eyes watered.

"You look good," he said hoarsely.

"I don't, but then again, I have cancer. This isn't a beauty contest." I had taken extra care to pencil on my eyebrows perfectly. I wore red lipstick, and added mascara to my few growing-in lashes. I had on foundation and blush. I didn't look healthy, but I wasn't ghastly. I couldn't face him looking truly wretched, knowing he was going back to his perfect blond wife and their perfect blond baby boy after lunch.

"Tara has grown up so much," he offered, taking a sip from his water glass. They'd tried to spend some time together.

"Children do that. Especially when you haven't seen them in years," I murmured, looking at the menu. I settled on a bowl of soup and a salad.

"I guess she told you things didn't go all that well today." He had taken her, alone, to lunch.

I nodded. "Did you expect otherwise?"

He shrugged. "I guess not." Did I hear in his voice a faint British clip? Was he really becoming a fake Brit, à la Madonna?

"Noah is almost eight now," I reported.

"Time flies." He shook his head and scanned the menu. I guessed he would order a steak and a salad.

Our waiter came over. "May I offer you a drink while you consider the menu?"

"I think we're ready to order." I smiled. "I'll have a tossed salad with oil and vinegar and a bowl of your corn chowder for my meal."

"And for the gentleman?"

"I'll have the filet mignon, cooked well-done, and a beefsteak tomato salad."

"Excellent. And to drink?"

I ordered a martini, and as I expected, he ordered a Dewar's on the rocks. Some things don't change. Knowing that, I felt certain wife number two would end up as abandoned as I had been. Which served her right. I was comforted by the thought that I could see it happening. Like a gypsy fortune-teller with my scarf on my head, I saw it all. The sobbing, the clinging, the begging him to stay even though it meant losing every last shred of dignity. Clutching the baby at night, wondering where she went wrong, how she had not seen it coming. Anger filling the place where heartache resided. Seeping through her like a sponge mops up a spill on the counter. Then, after a while, the empty hollow, neither anger nor love residing there, just empty space.

"So I suppose you're here to talk about the kids, though coming all the way to London is a little over the top, even for you, Lily."

I felt the knife twisting in me. I stared across the table. How had I ever been married to a man who would undermine my very being at every turn, make me doubt my sanity? I remembered all the nights he hadn't come home from NYU, how he'd "fallen asleep in his office." I knew. I wasn't one of those women…the last to know. The signs were there, and yet when I confronted him, he assured me it was all in my head. I was only imagining that when he touched me in bed, in my pregnant state, that he was secretly repulsed. I only imagined that making love was robotic, his eyes shut, where once they had stared down at me, full of fire. But maybe the fire had been imagined, too. I knew what he ate. I knew what he drank. But I had no access to his heart and soul. Never had. And neither did Child Bride. She was someone new to manipulate. I felt a tiny bit sorry for her. Just a tiny bit.

"Look, David, it's clear your involvement with the children is minimal. It's too much effort to call them, even on their birthdays. Months and months go by without them hearing from you."

"Lily, I have an important position here. I have responsibilities to my new family. To my in-laws."

"Ah, yes, Lord and Lady Marlborough. Cheerio, old chap."

"Don't mock, Lily. I always hated how you mocked everything."

"I always hated how you fucked everything."

"Is that what's brought you here? Across the Atlantic? To hash out imagined affairs and water under the bridge?"

Our drinks arrived, and I swallowed half of mine and signaled for another. I felt like I was losing my footing.

"You complain about the child support."

"Well, I have a life here. And I feel like I'm sending tremendous support to you, and I don't know what you spend it all on."

"Oh—" I looked down at my nails "—you know, frivolous things. Food, a glove for Little League, a roof over their heads, school supplies, savings for college. Nothing important, David."

"Again the mocking."

"Do you even care about them, David?"

His voice dropped an octave. "Keep your voice down. Of course I do. I love my children very much, but I can't help that I live so far away from them."

I shook my head. I had the urge to pick up my steak knife and plunge it into his jugular.

"I'm dying, David."

I watched him blink rapidly, three or four times in succession, then he exhaled and leaned back in his chair, his shoulders sagging. It was like watching a balloon deflate.

"I don't know what to say. I'm sorry."

"Spare me."

"I am. I knew you had cancer, I just had no idea. I thought you'd have chemo and get better."

"What could you know, David? What can you *possibly* know about throwing your guts up all day long, and then reading bedtime stories at night, being both a mother and father. Pulling over to the side of the road to throw up on the way to soccer practice, smiling through the pain so your kids don't guess how bad it really is. You don't know because you haven't bothered to ask. Not once did you call to offer me your support. Not one phone call."

"It's not my place to give you support."

"Did you call *them* to make sure they were okay, knowing their mother had cancer?"

He didn't answer and looked away. When he looked back he sighed again, then drained his Dewar's in one smooth gulp.

"I want you to sign these papers, David." I pulled them from my purse. "I want the children to remain in the U.S. after I die."

"With who? Let me guess. Michael." He said Michael's name like it was bile in his throat. They'd both always been jealous of the other.

"Yes. Michael."

"He's not even family, Lily. He's not even a blood relative."

"He's the closest thing they have to a blood relative. Did you know he coaches Noah's baseball team? Takes Tara to track. Holds their hands when they're feverish. Makes them dinner. Does all the Dad things you should be doing but aren't."

"He's gay."

"Now *that's* a newsflash. Is he really?"

"The sarcasm again. I hate it!" He leaned forward and propped his elbows on the table and put his head in his hands. "This is not fair. You're hitting me with too much at once."

"What's not fair is that I won't be around to watch

Tara graduate from high school or to dance at Noah's wedding. What's not fair, you self-centered bastard, is I have so little faith in you that I can't imagine them coming to live with you and Lizzie. That's what's not fair. They didn't even get a birth announcement when their half brother was born. They didn't even know Lizzie was pregnant. But then again, they're not thirty-seventh in line for the throne."

"That's not fair, and you know it."

"Cut the crap with the fair angle, David. Life isn't fair. Death isn't fair. It's not a level playing field."

Our salads arrived, along with my second drink. We immediately ordered another round.

"Fine. You know, it might be okay for Tara, I mean she'll be off to college in a couple of years anyway. But do you really think I can stand by and watch my son be raised by a faggot?"

My fork was raised. His hand was on the table. I could have reached over and impaled him.

"Better than a deadbeat, David."

"So what are these papers?"

"You waive your parental rights. The child support stops now. End of story. When they're each eighteen, if they're so inclined, they can look you up. You can keep in touch, if you want. But Michael becomes their legal guardian." I pressed the papers down onto the crisp white tablecloth. They lay halfway between the two of us, in no-man's-land.

"What would people think, Lily? A man giving up his children? It's just not done."

"And so you'd have them come here to live with you and Lizzie and baby royal?"

"No. They can stay in America with Michael. But I don't want to sign any formal papers."

"I can't risk that you'll have a fit of guilt after I die and change your mind. You have to sign them."

"Let me have the papers, and I'll think it over. Have my attorney look at them. You're asking me to say I don't love my own children. That they're not mine."

"I'm not." I felt tears and rubbed at my eyes, smearing my pathetic little lashes. "I'm asking you to love them enough to know they don't have a place in your world anymore, but they do have a place with Michael."

I pushed the papers across the table, closer to him. They were thick and folded in thirds.

"Sign them, David. If you really do love them, sign them."

He looked at me across the table. "I can't. I may not be a perfect father, but I am their father, and I can't sign away that right."

My next martini arrived. I wished to be held by Pete. I wanted to talk to Michael. I sipped and thought of my next move. Tara's and my plane left the next day. This was my only chance. He looked so sincere. I was asking him to do the unthinkable. But I pushed that down.

I remembered the night he came to the hospital after Noah was born. "I need to tell you that when you come home from the hospital, I won't be there." He confessed that the snowstorm he was stranded in had just given him another night with Lizzie. It had been going on the entire time I was pregnant. *No, crying won't change things. I'm not in love with you anymore. No, the baby doesn't change anything. No. No. No.* I remembered this as I brought out my final weapon. My last chance.

"Does Lizzie know we slept together in New York? After you two were married?"

"You wouldn't, Lily. You wouldn't." His voice registered horror.

He had flown to Manhattan five years ago to do a guest lecture and asked me to meet him. He was just in town for a night before he headed on to Denver to visit with a colleague. I brought along Tara's latest report card and some recent snapshots. I was between boyfriends, and part of me never got over not saying goodbye. That he had left without closure—whatever that was. Lawyers had handled it all, and I never felt like I had properly shut the door on the man I once loved, even if I came to understand that I loved an image. A smart deceiver masquerading as a husband.

We drank wine. Lots of it. And before I knew it, we were having a nightcap in his room. When he leaned over to kiss me, to say he was sorry for the hurt he'd caused, and I felt the lips of my children's father on my neck, I had a night of insanity. We'd made love, but for me it was a goodbye fuck. A last time to put it all to rest. It wasn't that I forgot the hurt and anger and rage, it was just that, for a night, I felt that slip away and in its place came a bittersweet farewell. After he fell asleep, I looked at him in the half dark. The bathroom light was on, casting half his face in light, half in shadow. That was David.

Half a creature of decency, the man I fell in love with, half a man consumed by his own need to be adored. I didn't adore him enough. I was too caustic, too sarcastic, too much a writer with a fresh mouth and a ready one-liner. I kissed him on the cheek and said goodbye on my terms and never looked back. It took me a month to tell Michael I had done something so stupid.

Now, here in London, the night that perhaps for him had been a bittersweet goodbye as well was going to cost him his children.

"Lily…that night was just—I don't know, a way of ending what was between us in the right way. I felt bad about what I had done. In the hospital…while you were pregnant. I didn't intend for us to be together that night." Panic edged his voice.

"Does she know?" I asked evenly.

He leaned back, staring at me in disbelief as the waiter cleared our salads and brought our dinner. He made no move to touch his steak. His face, his strong, broad cheekbones, were deathly pale. Like me without my layer of makeup.

"They're my children, too. This is blackmail, Lily. You can't do this. Not this way. Let me think about it."

I looked at the papers on the table between us. "Sign them."

"No."

"Fine." I pulled my cell phone from my purse.

"What does that mean? You don't have the balls to call Lizzie. You don't."

"I don't have the time to wait for you to sign them.

I don't have time to waste, David. Time is what I do not have, and you're asking me for time. Now I'm *telling* you I will do whatever it takes to make sure my children are cared for after I am gone. Lizzie will not raise them. Lizzie and her uppercrust family will have nothing to do with Noah and Tara. Yesterday with Tara was a failure. You saw that. She and Lizzie can't even share a meal together. I will not waste five minutes hesitating. I will call her. I don't have a choice."

"This is evil, Lily. What you're doing is evil."

I shrugged. "Sometimes evil is born of necessity."

I ate my soup in silence. He didn't touch his food. After a while, he lifted the papers and began reading them. I bent my head over my soup, occasionally glancing at him. He rubbed his eyes with his right hand. Tears. I calmly ate my soup, forcing myself to think of Christmas. No card. No presents. Noah's fifth birthday. When the child support check came that month there was an extra twenty-five dollars and a note in the memo portion of the check, in David's handwriting, "Happy Birthday Noah." Tears could not move me. Not today. I didn't have time.

His steak lay untouched as he stood. "I can't. I have to go see Noah. If I lose Lizzie, I lose her. But I don't think I will."

I had a sinking feeling. He was so certain he wouldn't lose her just as my real self told me I couldn't call Child Bride. Our night together to say goodbye would remain our secret. Maybe it was because I once loved him. I was defeated.

"How long do you have?"

"Months, maybe. Maybe a year."

"Will Michael keep in touch with me?"

"That's up to you. You call. He'll talk to you. You can call the kids."

"That night meant something to me. I do have regrets, Lily. I loved you very much at one time."

I looked down at my plate. "Me, too. You're part of my children."

"What do I owe you for dinner?"

"Nothing."

"Just my children, right?" He stood and threw his napkin down.

"No. Just take the papers and think about it," I whispered. "I won't call her. I think you know me better than I thought you did."

"The Lily I knew wouldn't hurt Lizzie. She was really young when I met her. I shouldn't have gotten involved with her. And I didn't tell her I was married. It's me you're mad at."

He leaned down and kissed me familiarly on the cheek, stood, turned and left, never looking back, his pace quickening as he got to the door of the restaurant. He stepped out and was gone into the grayish London night.

26

Michael

Pete was good for Lily. And he and I worried together while she was gone. Lily's oncologist was furious because the trip could literally threaten Lily's life. But arguing with her was futile. I let her go, helped out with picking Noah up from school and spent more time with George.

"I could get used to this." He smiled at me Saturday night, as I sat at the end of the bar waiting for him to finish in the kitchen. His manager was going to close that night. Then we drove to my place and parked on the street.

"I rented *Philadelphia Story*," I told him as we walked to my apartment. The air was typical New York spring, couldn't decide whether to be cold and miserable or warm…so it was a cross between the two, warm, with chilly breezes.

In my apartment, I poured two glasses of merlot and set up the VCR. George looked at the photos on my desk and on the bookshelves. He did that every time he came over. I wondered if it was a nervous habit.

"When can I meet Lily's kids?" he asked.

"Soon," I said. "I thought maybe we could all try to go to a Yankee game."

"Sounds great," he said, but he looked away.

"What?" I sat down on the couch.

"I don't feel like I really belong. You have this family life, sort of. It's strange, don't you think?"

I didn't think so. Maybe I used to, but I stopped trying to classify love.

"No," I said flatly.

"I don't mean it in a bad way."

"Yes, you do. Like what is a queer doing with a straight woman and a pair of kids?"

"No…I guess I just wonder where I fit in."

"Same place you have since I met you. You said yourself when we started that you're married to your job."

He paced nervously back and forth. We both knew we were about to have our first fight. That's a test, isn't it? The first fight, the first make-up session, the first time one of you cheats or does something low. The first time you meet each other's parents. That would be rich. My mother would shriek, and my father wouldn't come out of the basement.

"I'm not. I am in a way, but I have time for you. I make time for you."

"Look, let's not make this a big deal. I have a hard enough time being in a relationship without a lot of strings and whining attached."

"I'm not whining," he whined.

"You are."

"Maybe I'd better go home. I'm tired from work. I shouldn't have said anything." He put on his jacket again. His face was pale. It made me want to hold him.

"Look, George, I've known Lily since we were in our twenties. I'm not running out on her or those kids now, just because I happened to have fallen in love."

As soon as I said it, you could have heard a pin drop in my apartment. I had blurted it out. Had I meant it? I felt feverish suddenly, like my face was flushed. Never, never, never give the other person in a new relationship the upper hand. What the fuck had I just done? Could I take it back? Did I want to? I slugged back my glass of merlot and poured another.

"I love you, too," he said and looked at the ground. Even playing field. I breathed a sigh of relief.

"Well…" I smiled. I shook my head, well… What do you say now? I stretched and got up from the couch.

I pulled him in my arms and kissed the top of his head. Next thing I knew we were in the bedroom. He was such a vulnerable lover. Maybe that was why I felt my stomach lurch each time we had sex.

He fell asleep before I did. I loved him. What do you know? It was like trying a new pair of five hundred dollar loafers on for size. Five hundred dollar loafers are a hell of a commitment. You have to try them on, walk around, see how they fit. But they do fit. They feel comfortable right away. But are they practical? George and I were completely impractical right now. And I loved him.

I slipped out of bed and went into the living room. I hadn't heard from Lily. I looked at my watch. It would be 8:30 in the morning in London. I called the St. Regis and they patched me through to her room.

"Hello-o-o-o?" Her voice was dry and groggy.

"Lily? It's Michael. What's going on?"

"I can't talk. Tara spent the day with him yesterday, and it didn't go well. I'll tell you more when I come home."

"What did he say about the kids?"

"We had dinner alone. He's such a fucking coward. When he saw me in my scarf...out of breath...he started welling up. Said it was too hard to see me this way. Like this is about *him* after all this goddamn time. And he didn't sign. He wants to come see Noah first. Seems he'd be willing to let Tara stay in New York, but...Noah's a different story. He's such a Spawn."

"I love George."

"What?"

"I love him. I told him tonight."

"Oh my God!" she squealed.

We shifted gears instantly. Real friendship is like the tides. It ebbs and flows, it fills the little trenches we build in our hearts. It finds our holes and fills them, then it seeps down deep. It washes up starfish and shells and magical things that we get excited about, like pieces of sea glass. And it washes up seaweed and man-o'-war and ugly things we'd rather have stay in the sea. It cleanses, and it goes on forever."

"I know," I whispered. "I feel like a kid. I'm not sure if I've ever felt this way."

"It's about time you grew up."

"We had a fight tonight."

"About what?"

"About the kids. You. He wonders where he fits in."

"I can't blame him."

"I don't have an answer for him, though. It's like I have two halves of myself. The you half and the him half. Only it's not fifty-fifty. He gets less of me. But that's just how it is."

"Michael, if I didn't have cancer, and I didn't have Peter, it would be me with this problem, not you. It's figuring out how to carve up a life and share it. You'll work it out."

"That Pete's a good guy. He called twice to check on the kids."

"He is a great guy. Listen, I don't want to talk right now. I want Tara to sleep in. Then we're going to go on a double-decker bus. We're leaving this afternoon. Wish me a safe flight."

"Pete will see you at the airport."

I hung up the phone and thought about Lily and Spawn. What he didn't realize, what he couldn't know, is that when it came to their kids, *her* kids, she would kill. If she had to drown him and sink him in the

Thames with weights on his ankles, she would. I almost felt bad for the guy. Sooner or later, he'd sign. But my sympathy was fleeting. Very fleeting.

I stood up and looked out the window. Ellie was with Noah. The view from my apartment was lousy. Mostly I could see the street below. There's a bar down on the corner so even at three-thirty in the morning, it was sort of busy. There was a night Michael and a day Michael, a drive Noah to school Michael and a lover Michael. A Michael for my lover and one for Lily. I just hoped my head and heart were big enough for both of me.

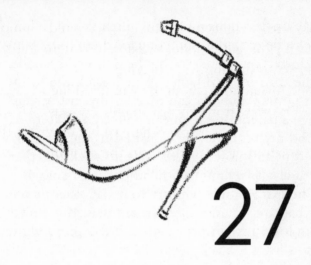

27

A Daughter's Turn
by Tara Waters

My mother asked me to write her column today.
Kind of like a school project.

My mom has cancer. When I tell people that,
they look at me like they feel really sorry for me.
When they find out my father lives in London and
I never see him, and my favorite uncle, Michael, is
gay, they think I have three heads. Add a pesky kid
brother and you have a teenager's nightmare.

But I decided to write about my family for this
column because family isn't about having everything picture-perfect. I'm not even sure I would
want everything perfect. Why? Well, my mom has
shown me that having cancer isn't the end of the
world, and you can have cancer and still take care
of your family. Being sick can give you courage.

My uncle Michael has shown me that you don't have to be related to someone for them to be family. He gets on my nerves, but he is more of a father to me than my real father. Which leads me to my next point. Anybody can have a baby. Just because you're a parent doesn't mean you're good at it.

And my brother…he's a pain. But my mom has raised us to know that we have to stick together. She is always telling us how important family is.

There are people who try to make other people feel bad for having different families. But isn't it about love? I mean, does God care whether a white person loves a black person? Or if two men love each other? Or if a Jewish person loves a Christian?

I don't think God cares *who* you love. He just cares *that* you love.

My mom having cancer helped me figure some of this out.

So even though my life isn't perfect—and believe me being a teenager is really hard these days—I still like my life. Most days. But don't tell my mom. She might make me clean my room.

28

Lily

This is a list of questions I have for the Big Man Upstairs when I die. I've been compiling them ever since I got sick. I have a notepad, and as I think of a question, I write it down. I don't know why, since I can't take the notepad to heaven—or wherever it is we go. Still I have them. For some reason, they help me.

1. Do they wear high heels in heaven? I've spent my life height-challenged, and I don't relish being the shortest angel in heaven. Are all angels the same height?

2. Why do bad things happen to good people? It's the unanswerable one here on earth. Finally, I want a straight answer.

3. Why is there cancer? What about poisonous snakes and cockroaches and really gross stuff? Why are some men evil? I mean like sociopathically evil? Were they born without a soul?

4. Why is a baboon's ass that funny red, and why is there that one ape with the funny nose, that big schnoz? I mean, some of the things in nature…kind of weird. Did you make them that way on purpose? Does a baboon's red ass show you, God, have a sense of humor?

5. Why do you allow children to be born to people who abuse them and not allow children to be born to infertile couples who desperately want kids?

6. Why is a good man hard to find?

7. Will leg warmers ever come into fashion again?

8. Is Satan real?

9. Is Satan related to my ex-husband? All right…I take that back.

10. Why do kids always know the *minute* you sit down on the toilet and predict that precise moment to come ask you a question? Do they have some sort of radar built in?

11. Is the reason you make babies so cute so that parents learn to love them before they reach the awful teenage stage?

12. Do you, Lord, really have a problem with gay people? Come on…really?

13. Do you really talk to televangelists and tell them stuff, like to run for president? I could probably cross this one out. I think I already know the answer.

14. Will my children forget me?

15. Do dogs go to heaven?

16. What about lesser animals, like cockroaches and the aforementioned poisonous snakes? How about gorillas?

17. Can animals talk to each other?

18. What's with Mother Nature—hurricanes, tsunamis, earthquakes? And is the world ever going to end?

19. So, was it the Big Bang?

20. Is the shroud of Turin real?

21. What is the secret to a perfect martini?

22. Why did I have to meet Pete after I got sick? Is fate real? Are you messing with us sometimes?

23. Who do you think is funnier? Leno or Letter-man?

24. Are you a man or a woman?

25. Finally...why do I have to die before I'm old?

29

Michael

Opening day.

What is it about baseball that makes grown men rhapsodize?

It's no secret I adore the game. Maybe because it was a way of communicating with a distant father, a product of the 1950s, a man watching control slip away from him in the turmoil of the '60s and '70s. Amid the familiar rhythm of playing catch, we didn't have to speak. We could just be: father and son.

Maybe the reason is the boys of summer. The idea that grown men can make a living doing what little boys love to do. They can put on their uniforms and jog out onto freshly mowed grass, baselines painted white, punch their gloves and throw the ball. They can live a fantasy for the rest of us working stiffs who have to grab the subway to work or jostle along the crowded streets, stuffed into shirts and ties. They passed up wingtips for cleats. Briefcases for gloves. Papers and legal briefs, or jackhammers and nails, for dust kicked up on the pitcher's mound.

Perhaps it's the ritual of the game I love. Watching the ticket-taker rip my ticket in half and hand me the stub for my scrapbook. Going to my seat and watching the guy clean it with a whisk broom for a tip and a smile. Ordering peanuts, lousy hot dogs and a beer, all of which now cost more than the tickets. Still, at the seventh-inning stretch, it's as if time stands still.

Is it the innocence we long for? The days when we picked sides by choosing captains and doing rock-paper-scissors to see who would bat first. Do we long for the uncomplicated? Do we long for a time when we played until the sun went down and games were called on account of darkness—or Mom's voice ringing out that dinner was on the table?

This season, for me, is particularly poignant. Baseball is all of those things for me. But this year has been the hardest of my life, I think. This year has been about loss and grief, about love and loneliness. It has been about learning what the word "family" really means, and that "I love you" is more than three little words mumbled in the darkness. This year, I think I finally grew up. And it was harder than I ever could have imagined.

I measure my life from baseball season to baseball season. Sometimes I measure a good day or bad one by how the Yankees did at bat. But now, more often than not, good days and bad days are calculated in different, more excruciating ways. So this season, I will look to get lost in the game, to escape for nine innings into a world of dandelions on a Little League field of dreams. Lost in a world that makes sense.

You see, baseball is also, for all its poetry and beauty, about statistics. There are rules. If you pitch the ball inside the batter's box and the batter misses, it's a strike. Outside…a ball. A few of those, you have a walk. There are RBI's and pitching stats. It is controlled. Sure, sometimes the ump makes a bad call. There's the occasional fight on the field. Back in childhood pickup games, there's even such a thing as a do-over.

But life's not like that.

Right now I have no do-overs. And a lot of what I'm going through makes no sense. I can't look up something in a rule book. I can't ask the ump. I can't ask my pitching coach. It's life. Not a game.

So opening day arrived for Noah. And so did Spawn. We got to the field and there he was, a few weeks after Lily's trip to London. He sat in the stands. With a Mets baseball cap on—his first mistake. I recognized him right away, but Noah didn't. Maybe it was the incongruence of his dad being there. But Noah took to the field. Pete was there too, standing off to the side. Lily was home in bed. And Spawn watched his son play.

I was pretty busy. Little League, at Noah's age, means keeping them focused on the game and not on who brought the snack and what's the snack and when do we get to eat the snack…the snack is pretty fucking important.

Before the boys took the field, I pulled Noah over.

"Noah…your dad's in the stands." It seemed like the right thing to do to get Noah to wave. Man, I was glad Lily wasn't there, though 'cause she would have ripped David a new one—he hadn't told her he was coming. I kind of guessed that was a bad sign. Like maybe he was going to try to take Noah back to London with him or something.

Noah looked in the direction I pointed and gave an unenthusiastic wave. Then he went out to his shortstop position, and I did what I always did. I kept them focused on the ball and not on the snack that Mrs. Connor brought. I had a bunch of kids to keep track of—and then two of them had to pee, so Pete took them over to the concession stand, which had a restroom in it.

I tried to coach them and remind them to throw to first, throw to first, throw to first. It's my mantra. Hey, we start with the basics.

So we played the whole game, and I was only vaguely aware of Spawn. Then it was snack time. Then passing out notices about the next game. Parents collected their kids, and finally, finally, I brought Noah over to his father.

Noah stuck out his hand, like a little gentleman. His father bent over to hug him, and Noah let him in the way a kid won't resist a hug from his great-aunt Gertrude, who's ninety-nine and has a mustache, although the kid is cringing inside.

"You played well, Noah. I know you must be surprised to see me."

Noah shrugged, then looked up at me. "Can Pete take me for a soda?"

"Don't you want to talk to your dad? Maybe go for something to eat."

"No, let him go," David said. "I was hoping to talk with you anyway, Michael."

So Noah scampered off to Pete. "What's up, David? You can't have stopped here by accident."

"No. I wasn't sure what I would find here. But I brought these." He handed me a legal envelope.

"What's this?"

"They belong with you, Michael. I saw it."

"Saw what?"

"He's part of you. He doesn't make a move, doesn't run a base or punch his glove, without looking over to you adoringly, making sure you approve. And you…you let him know you love him with every wink, every glance, the way you wave him home at third."

"It's just baseball, David."

"No. It's life."

"Maybe, but you're still his father."

"I know, but I can't do this. I don't want to do this. That's the thing. I even got a vasectomy after Drew was born. I don't have it in me. I love them, but I love my world the way it is even more. I guess…I turned out to be the selfish one after all."

"Are you sure?"

He nodded. "That's why I came. To be sure. I sat here

Erica Orloff

for nine innings and knew I'd never even play catch with him. It's not who I am, Michael. I'll keep in touch." He stuck out his hand and then turned and walked across the field to his rental car. Looked like a rental anyway.

About ten minutes later, Noah came back with Pete. He didn't ask where his father was. He only said, "Come on. Let's go. I'm hungry."

I shrugged, and we went back to Lily's house. She was sleeping upstairs. I tiptoed up there and cracked the door.

"Hmm?" She rolled over sleepily.

"David was at Little League."

"*My* David?"

"Well, technically he hasn't been that in a long while."

"Shut up. You know what I mean."

"Yes, your David. Spawn."

"What did he want?" The panic in her voice was palpable.

"To give you these." I put the papers on the bed. Maybe he wasn't the Spawn of Satan after all.

And then I saw it. She relaxed. She finally relaxed for the first time since her diagnosis. She touched the envelope like it was a holy relic.

"Thank you," she whispered out loud. I wasn't sure to whom.

30

Goodbye
by Lily Waters

This is my last column. I'm taking a leave of absence, and I'm not sure if I'll be back. My hair is back, after chemo, and it's curly—without a perm! But I'm afraid cancer is in my lungs and there's also a suspicious spot on my brain. So it's time to take a break from the column. Or, more specifically, from my editor Joe, who is an ornery type of the old school of journalism, but who taught me an awful lot in my years here.

I wanted to also say a few things before I go. For one thing, having cancer does not make you brave. It doesn't. It makes you sick. I know it's terribly romantic to sort of picture me lying in bed like the dying Camille, looking ethereal and beautiful, my new-grown hair splayed out. But dying is really an ugly business, and I would greatly prefer not to be doing it.

Another thing. David Letterman once asked Warren Zevon, the great rock and roller, when he was dying of cancer, what he knew. The ever sarcastic rocker said something about taking time to eat more good sandwiches or something like that. At the time, I kind of thought it was a smart-alecky thing to say. But since then, I've realized a few things. One of them is that people who are dying really don't have a handle on any great theory. It's not like I can tell you whether the Big Bang theory is correct, whether the shroud of Turin is real or why bad things happen to perfectly wonderful people.

However, Zevon was right. It is about the sandwiches. And the hugs. And the ordinary. It's about that moment you wish you could preserve forever, when your kids are laughing uproariously, as only kids can, with wild abandon, and you're smiling, and thoughts of bills and grown-up responsibilities are miles away. It's those moments that are heaven on earth. Dying just makes you realize it. You realize it's about the love and not much else.

You discover, when you're dying, that he who has the most toys at the end does not win. Nope. He who has someone, like I do, to hold their hand as they go gently into this good night…they win.

If I were to die tomorrow, I leave a house with a leaky roof, a pile of credit card debt and a dog who eats me out of house and home and who has bad gas. I also leave, I hope, love.

I have loved my editor Joe—yeah, ornery old saw that he is.

I have loved my best friend Michael. I've written enough over the years about him that to say anything more would be redundant. I promise to find out for him what happened when disco died. Did it get to go to heaven?

I have even loved my ex-husband. Because the closer you get to death, the more you realize that even though people disappoint you, they usually are doing the best they can—and that even lost love is beautiful in its own poignant way.

I have loved Pete. It was my luck to meet a great guy at the least convenient time. But that's me. Always about bad timing.

And finally, I have loved Noah and Tara. It all comes down to them. The one love that is so large it consumes you, in a way, so that you cease to be this entity unto yourself and instead have this cosmic umbilical cord forever binding them to you, heart to heart.

Oh, and maybe one more thing. I have lived. I mean, yes, I have lived and breathed. But beyond that, I lived with passion each and every day. I was type A, driven to live on the edge, feel it all, love it all. When I was younger I loved hard, played hard. I have grabbed on to life like a rodeo rider grabbing on to that crazy bull—the killer one everyone else is too scared to sit astride. And man…I have ridden it for all it's worth. I have no regrets.

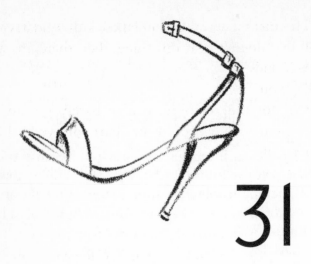

31

Michael

It seems like love is all about labels: gay or straight? Married or just shacking up? I had no label for Lily's and my friendship. I had no label for how I felt about George. I just called both of them love. George didn't see it that way.

We had just finished a dinner we cooked together at my place. Two steaks, broiled to medium-rare, delicious red potatoes in an herbed butter, asparagus steamed with orange juice. A bottle of Australian Shiraz. Chocolate éclairs. Then I told him.

At first, he just gripped the arm of the couch. Then he stood and paced. "How can you expect me to accept that, Michael?" His eyes welled up.

I stood up, too. Facing him. "Look, George, before you

and I ever met there was Lily and these kids. And if, God forbid, Lily doesn't beat this thing, then there are still those two kids."

"Why you?"

"Why not me? George, you've barely gotten to know them. They could be part of your life, too…our life."

"But I have no interest in playing Daddy. I have a restaurant to run. I barely have time to see you as it is, and if this came to pass, Michael, you'd be split in half. Half for me, half for them. Oh…and the half for your job, and the half for the Yankees. The half for your mother. There's not enough halves to go around."

"You make it sound like I'm a stock commodity. Shares traded on Wall Street. Well, I'm not. I'm me, George. Complicated, maybe, but life is complicated."

"Not this complicated."

"George, this is a formality, and chances are this will never come to pass because Lily is not going to die."

His voice trembled as he whispered, "You need to stop lying to yourself, Michael. Anyone can take one look at her and know it's only a matter of time. She wouldn't have suggested this if she didn't know deep down inside, herself, that she wasn't going to make it. She knows, Michael, and I'll say it because you won't. She's *dying!*"

Without even thinking, I slapped him. Me, throwing a fit like a diva. I don't pull stunts like this in relationships—not, mind you, that I was ever very serious with anyone before George. But I slapped him.

He stood there, stunned, his face careening from one

emotion to the next: shock, horror, anger and finally, a flood of tears.

"George, don't…" I moved toward him, my arms outstretched. "I'm so sorry…"

"No, *you* don't," he screamed, grabbed his coat and rushed from my apartment, not looking back. I didn't know whether to follow him or wait for him to cool down, so I watched him leave, my insides a jumble. The door slammed like a final exclamation point. A slam of "You blew it, Michael."

I sat down on my couch and dialed the telephone. I called his answering machine, feeling myself get teary at the sound of his voice, "This is George, leave a message and have a peaceful day." God, I loved his voice. "George, I'm under a lot of stress, and I just lost my head, man. I'm sorry. I can't imagine losing you, and I'm hoping we can work through this." I hung up.

I don't know if I ever thought of myself as a happily ever after guy. Even if I could legally marry a man, I had never thought about marrying any of the guys I'd been with. I had trouble, with my attention span, getting past breakfast. Until I met George.

It wasn't his looks, or even the sex. It was the other stuff. Watching movies together, cooking together, going to a ball game or just hanging out. The fact that we could fall into a silence that was as comfortable as my Yankee jacket. And I had stopped thinking about when we might grow bored of each other. I had started thinking in terms of, if not forever, then a long, long time. Why had I slapped him?

Was it because George had told me what no one else has the courage to say? Had I not seen the way the shadow was overtaking her?

George saw the shadow. He saw it hulking and looming, waiting. Sitting in my apartment, I felt cold. I wrapped my arms around myself. The shadow was rubbing its hands together, knowing, knowing time was on its side. Time was on the side of cancer. Time could wait out her energy and strength. It could wait out her resolve and her fight. It could wait out her spirit. Time and this shadow called death. They were best of friends. Coconspirators in the death trade.

I hadn't seen the shadow. I saw life. I saw her smile and heard her laughter. I argued with her over who was the better actress: Barbara Stanwyck or Joan Fontaine. She always chose Joan and so we argued. We all know it's Stanwyck. We popped popcorn. We watched movies. We went to soccer games. We went to Yankee games. I watched the sunlight over Yankee Stadium play on her face, dappling it in light, as the boys of summer ran the bases. I saw the light, not the shadow. I refused to see the shadow, as if not seeing might make it so.

George had seen the flicker of defeat. George had seen she had already lost. I saw her ruin scrambled eggs in the morning and heard her reading *The Hobbit* to Noah. I listened to her voice and heard her bravery, while George heard the weakness.

I turned off the lamp in the living room and sat in the dark. I didn't want the shadow of death to see me cry. I didn't want it to know I felt the cold. I prayed in the dark for a long time. I prayed for a miracle. I prayed for courage. I prayed I knew what I was doing with Noah and Tara. I prayed George would forgive me. I prayed to understand why there is the valley of the shadow of death. We walk this life in a dream, never realizing the valley is there. It's always far off, in the distance. We don't accept it. We turn our eyes from it. But it's there. It's quiet and still. It has time on its side.

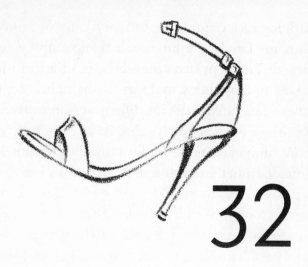

32

Lily

I don't know if Michael was ever in love before George. I know he was really close to Damon, years ago. Damon was a beautiful columnist from the paper with coffee-colored skin and a physique to match Michael's. Physically, I think you'd be hard-pressed to find two more beautiful men within a hundred-mile radius of Manhattan. Both of them inspired the usual comments from my female friends, "What a waste. The pair of them." Back then, I routinely tried matchmaking. And Michael and Damon elicited sighs from my potential fixer-uppers. I liked Damon a lot, too. He was funny and used to mock Michael's vanity as much as I did. He read eclectic authors and loved talking books. Michael would cook us all dinner and we'd stay up late debating politics and one-upping each other with stories of bad dates and the familiar "my family is more insane than yours."

Then Damon was diagnosed HIV-positive, and Michael said he couldn't handle it. We had buried eight friends already at that point. Not just acquaintances. *Friends.* They were people we loved. We watched families shut out gay lovers from funerals. Our friend Tom was evicted from the apartment he shared with his lover and his lover's family wouldn't even give him his own clothes. Damon looked healthy, but that was when HIV was a death sentence. I know Michael really hurt Damon. I don't think he meant to abandon him. He was *always* a commitment-phobe. But Michael never dwelled on how he hurt others. He was Michael. Center of his own handsome universe. Love wasn't part of his vocabulary, except with me. Sort of that "Love ya, you big idiot," kind of love, where I half expected him to punch me in the arm when he said it. But when he and George split up, I had never, not in twenty years, seen him such a mess.

"I don't fucking get how selfish he's being...." Michael leaned over his wineglass, his eyes squeezed shut. Tissues were sprawled, crumbled on my bed.

"Maybe he just needs time—"

"Time? To accept that I am suddenly going to be a father? I don't think all the time in the fucking world is going to fix that, Lily. And why? Am I different because I am involved with Noah and Tara? I always have been. Why does a little thing like formalizing it make it different? Am I different? Do I look different to you? Do I?"

He sat on my bed, cross-legged, wine bottle on my nightstand. He was now two glasses into bottle number two. Noah and Tara were in their rooms, Noah asleep, Tara on the phone.

"It's a lot for him to grasp. But really, Michael, I'm sure he loves you."

"Don't use that word."

"Why not?"

"Just don't."

"Why? He does. And I know you love him, too. Did you remind him of that?"

He shrugged, then tossed back his glass of wine. He was looking at a killer hangover tomorrow. Then again, that's how I always felt lately. No matter how I tried to get comfortable, I ached, as if I had the worst flu on record. Yet I never hated cancer for what it did to me. How crazy is that? I hated it for what it did to the people around me. If I hadn't so desperately needed Michael to be guardian of the kids, George and he would be happily together.

"Come on, you stubborn ass, put your head down," I coaxed. "This will all work out. I know it. I know you and George are meant to be together."

"I hate him."

"You don't." I patted the pillow next to mine. "Come on. You look terrible. Let's watch an old movie, and I'll make some popcorn."

"You'll burn it."

"I'll try not to."

Michael at last put his head down. I'd been watching

him drink and listening to him talk for over two hours. He took the remote—he is a total remote hog, like all men—and clicked over to the old movie channel.

"*Rebecca*! Oh my God, it's just starting. Go make popcorn."

I was tired, but I forced myself out of bed and down to the kitchen. I burned the first bag of microwave popcorn by turning the bag wrong-side down. The second bag had that terrible burned-popcorn smell, but the top two-thirds of the popcorn in the bag was yellow and unburned. So I put the good popcorn in a bowl, picked out a few brown ones and went back upstairs. Michael was snoring heavily. His face was unlined. I shook my head. He must have struck a bargain with the devil to look that good for this long. I glimpsed my face in my dresser mirror. My eyebrows had returned, but one of my other medicines now made me puffy. I wasn't winning any beauty pageants.

I covered Michael with a quilt and went down the hallway and picked up the phone in my study. I called George's restaurant and asked for him. I've been a meddler all my life.

"Hello?"

"George, it's Lily," I whispered.

He was silent. So I plunged ahead. "Michael doesn't know I'm calling. He's so miserable without you, George. Please reconsider. Please. I know it's all so new—*we're* all so new—but please think about it."

"Lily, I like you. I like the children, but…I can't talk. I have a restaurant to run. You see? I am so busy. He is so busy. If he's a father, that's just less time I have for me. Us. I don't know if I can handle that. I'm very set in my ways." He was quiet. I could hear the bustle of the restaurant in the background.

"You know, don't you?"

"Know what?"

"What he won't face. That he really will be a single father."

"I see it. I see you."

I thought what George was essentially saying would hurt me, but I was somehow relieved that someone, anyone, was looking at me with truth. I was dying. "He loves you, George," I offered.

George didn't respond. "I have to go, Lily."

"He does."

"Goodbye."

He hung up the phone, and I listened to dead air for a while. Then I hung up. Michael needed George. George, I knew, needed him. Somehow, they just fit. I would just have to make them realize it.

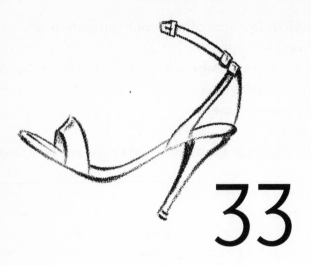

33

Michael

Lily had a long list of do's and don'ts for her funeral. She wanted me to give the eulogy. She wanted Pete to sit with me and the kids. She wanted my mother in the second row with Joe. She wanted martinis served after at a party at her house. Also she liked these little canapés I make. She also made me promise to play Bruce Springsteen. No hymns. No open casket—she preferred cremation. Then she wanted her urn to sit on the fireplace next to a picture of her. If that creeped us out too much, she asked me to scatter her ashes in the shoe department of Macy's. I told her the fireplace sounded like a better option. She also said she wanted us to have lots of pictures of her looking gorgeous around. From back when we first met. Our vacation at

Club Med. Pictures of her and the kids when they were small.

She wanted to institute a No Crying rule at her funeral, but I didn't imagine it was enforceable. I assumed we had tons of time.

We didn't.

I thought death gave out warning signs, but sometimes, death doesn't. It enters in silence and leaves just as quietly.

This is the eulogy I gave:

I wish I could say that Lily died with all her friends around her, holding her hand, me right there. Joe barking at her. Her college roomie flown in. Pete. The kids. The dog at her feet.

But she didn't. I was there all morning. She was at home. And I sat next to her, just talking, sharing memories. And she said she was tired. Would I leave her to sleep? Then she was hoping to have a sandwich. So mundane. Tuna. On white toast. Cut the crusts off. Oh and would I mind making a little side salad with it. No croutons. I rolled my eyes and left her to rest.

When I came back, she wasn't breathing.

I can't tell you how much that bothered me, until I remembered this was *Lily* we were talking about. She'd want to do things *her* way. Not my way or your way. My guess is she thought it would be less crying. Less phlegm as she used to put it, if she was alone. I have no doubt she did it that way—which was kind of a Lily way of getting in the last word—on purpose.

And I haven't a doubt in my mind, she is already

up there in heaven, in her high heels, marching on a cloud, giving orders.

For those of you that knew her really well, you know arguing with her was pointless. She always got her way, about everything. Even the remote control—though she'll swear it was me who hogged it.

From the first time I met her when she almost burned down an entire city block trying to make chicken, to her determination to make it as a reporter and then a columnist. To her fashion sense when her hair came out with the chemo and she swore no wigs—only scarves. That she would start a new trend. Revive the gypsy look. She had a way of looking at the world that, I have to be honest, didn't always even make sense. But I never knew anyone who loved life more, or who was more determined to embrace each day.

Joe, her editor, read her last column to you. She tried to tell the world that embracing each day was a lesson learned while dying. It wasn't. It was a lesson learned while living. She didn't learn it because she was sick. She learned it because that was who she was.

And to her children, I can only say she loved you enough for many lifetimes. And it is my job to make sure you never forget her.

No open casket—that was her getting in the last word. Just that table of pictures. And that pair of high heels. I added them. Not because she wore high heels everywhere—even the soccer field—but because those shoes will remain impossible to fill.

She always believed she was height-challenged. But she never was. She lived life larger than all of us.

There wasn't a dry eye in the memorial chapel. Noah put on a brave face. I tried to. I was amazed at how full the place was. The entire staff of the paper. Her neighbors. Soccer moms. The Little League team. Even the guy where she bought her bagels.

Then two extraordinary things happened. Though given this was Lily we're talking about, maybe not so amazing.

First, George walked through the door of the chapel. He pulled me aside later at the house, apologized and told me we'd weather parenthood together, figure it out as we went along. He set about putting out the canapés and making martinis and doing what she wanted. Everyone listened to her. They were afraid not to.

Second, my father showed up as I was giving the eulogy.

I was dumbfounded. I mean, not only that he had shown up, but that he had gotten so damn old in the last twenty years. I saw pictures at my mother's, but he had, the stubborn old bastard, managed to avoid seeing me in the flesh all these years. If I went to a wedding, he didn't. And vice versa. I felt like I was seeing a ghost of him. This big, burly man I had once been so intimidated around was kind of a shell of his old self.

And he was crying. I mean big messy tears.

After I shook hands with the guests and got the kids settled with Pete into the limousine for the ride back to the house, I told them to go without me. I'd be right along. And I went over to my father, who was lingering in the back of the chapel looking out of sorts.

"Long time, no see," I said, kind of coldly.

"You could say that."

"What the hell are you doing here, Dad?"

"Your mother told me you became a father."

"Well…not exactly, Dad."

He waved his hand as if to stave off tears. I noticed his other hand had a letter in it. "No, no, I know that. But you've done an amazing thing taking on these kids."

I kept staring at his left hand. "What's that?"

"Nothing."

I recognized Lily's handwriting on the outside of the envelope.

"What are you doing with a letter from Lily, Dad?"

"Oh…I can't tell you. She made me promise. You know she used to come visit me from time to time. I wasn't supposed to tell you that either, but if she saw your mother, she made a point of coming into the den…. Eh…anyway, you better go, son."

I looked at him, still not really understanding what the hell he was doing there. And then, without warning, he grabbed me and pulled me to him and started crying into my shoulder.

"I'm so, so sorry."

I stiffened, but then the weight of everything sort of made me collapse and I softened into this hug.

I have no idea what the letter said. But I just figured it was like Lily to have the last word.

There was a lone limo waiting for me outside, and I settled into the backseat. Martinis. Canapés. Was she out of her mind at the end? Who would feel like having a party?

But when I got to the house, people were laughing. Drinking. Eating. Crying. But most of all, making noise. They were celebrating her life the way she wanted them to.

Lily lived a noisy life. A messy life. An organizationally-challenged one.

And as I looked around, it dawned on me she knew exactly what she was doing when she handed me her funeral plans.

I just wish she had given me a detailed plan for the rest of our lives. Because for *that,* I hadn't a clue as to what to do.

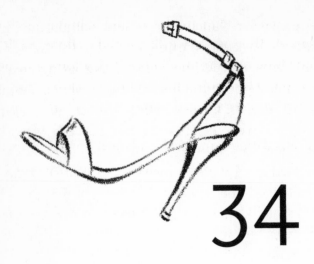

34

Michael

You don't realize how much of a hurricane someone is, until they leave. Maybe you picture their leaving, sort of like arriving at the eye of a storm, but until they are really gone, you don't really know the full devastation.

In the weeks after Lily died, me, Pete, George, Joe, Noah, Tara, Ellie—even my parents—were the walking wounded. My department chair, Martin, the guy who'd helped Lily with her surprise party for me, was, in the end, an even better guy than I could have imagined. He hurriedly put together a family leave for me and fast-tracked a sabbatical for the following semester.

Joe had taken to dropping by—a lot. As if the paper just wasn't fun anymore without her to argue with. He would sit in a chair in the living room, watching CNN.

Noah would come in and Joe would help him with his homework. But mostly, we all seemed to flounder. It all reminded me of a day in Central Park a long time ago. One of those days you think nothing of at the time, but then later, you see it laced with meaning.

She was dating a medical student who was offered a residency in L.A. He wanted her to come with him. She could pursue her writing there just as easily as New York. She didn't know what to do, so we went to Central Park with a blanket, bought two Italian ices and lazed in the dappled spring sunlight filtering through the trees.

I remember that it was one of those fluke days in March, when New York weather can't decide what it's going to do. One day it's icy cold, the next it can be this burst of spring, warm enough to wear a T-shirt and jeans, a light jacket, and maybe even flip-flops and let your toes sink into the just awakening spring grass a bit.

She finished her cherry Italian ice and had the ruby-red lips of a little kid, complete with a red stain from dripping ice down her chin. She laid back and stared up at the tree we were under.

"So I don't know whether to go."

"You're young. Life is full of possibility. You could go out there and break into screenwriting. Or get a job in the movie biz."

"I don't want to be a screenwriter. I want to be a newspaper writer."

"They have newspapers out there."

"I know. But don't you feel like New York is a part

of your heart? I can't picture living anywhere else. I mean, from the pretzel carts to the museums, to the clubs, to just the people and the energy, it's my home. And I don't know if I'm in love with Kyle enough to go clear across the United States."

I was sitting cross-legged and then unfolded my legs and rolled over on my stomach until we were almost nose to nose on the blanket. I looked at her, with those red ice stains and just shook my head. She was a piece of work. "You can always come back. That's what my mom used to tell me when I was afraid of something— like leaving for college or even sleepaway camp when I was young. I mean, you could go to L.A. just for the experience, and if you hate it, you can come back."

She huffed and pouted.

"What?"

"Nothing."

"Obviously I said something to piss you off. What?"

"It's just…I guess I want you to say that you don't want me to go."

I looked at her kind of confused. We were close friends, and we did a lot together, but I didn't have a *best* friend, in a sense. Not since Charlie—that was his real name. My novel was true. I was Sam. Trusting anyone, totally, again seemed impossible. Or so I thought.

"Well, that would be selfish of me."

"But you'd miss me."

"I don't know. I mean you have Kyle and it only makes sense that one day you'll get married and live your own life."

"But I always assumed you'd be part of it."

"Well…uh…" I faltered.

"I don't care what you say. You'd miss me."

"I mean, I would, but this is an opportunity for you."

"Say it, though. *You'd miss me.*"

"I…"

She stood up and twirled around, and in this ridiculous singsong voice, she started saying, "You'd miss me. You won't admit it, but you'd miss me."

I shook my head. She was crazy.

How could I miss such an exasperating woman?

How could I miss her so much it was like a piece of me was wrenched out of my insides?

Every day, I faced things I wanted to ask her about. So, she had known nothing about cooking—and frankly, she apparently knew nothing about how to iron. I found the household's lone iron in the garage behind a bag of rock salt. However, was there a secret to getting Tara to pick up her room, or to explaining the mysteries of chloroplasts to Noah for his science test? This stuff she apparently did without thinking was now something entirely new.

And Gunther was depressed, so I had a depressed gaseous dog on my hands.

George, God love him, was great. We were taking it slow, which meant he stayed over on Sunday nights and did carpool duty on Monday mornings. He cooked on occasion, and he showed Tara how to use one of his old 35-millimeter cameras to take black-and-white photos.

She seemed to use the pictures as a way to express her grief, because Lord knows she wasn't talking to me. She took stark pictures, finding scenes that weren't about death—but if you looked close, yeah. A lone bird on a telephone wire on a desolate street. A Coke can, crushed and discarded in a gutter. She talked to Justin—and she talked to Justin's mother, a wonderful woman, albeit a bit too New-Agey for me, but maybe that was what Tara needed. Tara had even taken to wearing a crystal Justin's mother got her on a velvet cord around her neck.

Noah…he cried a lot. I think it was an entire month before he didn't cry himself to sleep. Baseball saved him, saved me. Something about putting those ticks in the boxes and keeping score, about playing catch, visiting the batting cages up on Route 9W, it helped us both.

I sort of assumed Pete would disappear. He didn't have this long vested interest in the kids. But Lily, I have to say, was right about him. They hadn't had much time together, but he loved her completely. Cancer had a way of slicing through time and bullshit. And he was a teacher after all. He loved kids. So he remained a part of our lives, and he became a real friend to me.

And then there was my father.

I still don't know what was in that letter, but he visited us. He treated Noah and Tara like his own grandkids. Considering my sister will likely never have kids herself—too flaky—he embraced grandfatherhood.

David and Lizzie call more often. Well, David does. Once a month. He doesn't make an effort to say he'll come visit. He doesn't do more than a perfunctory check-in, I suppose. And someday, if they want, the kids can go to London for a visit. They can channel their cast-off feelings into anger or into photographs, like Tara. They can figure it out.

I miss her.

I sit here and I wonder how long it will be before I have a day without this imaginary conversation in my head. I seem to know her one-liners. Know what she would say. I see something funny and want to call and tell her.

She was a hurricane who stormed into my life perched on a pair of high heels.

And when the house is really quiet, I can almost hear her mocking me, like that day in the park.

"You'll miss me."

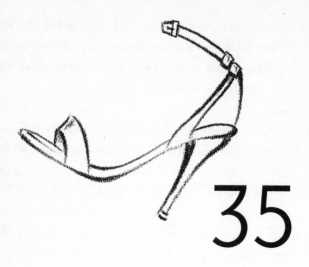

35

Lily

I saw them all.

At my funeral.

The funny thing is, all along I don't think I ever really pictured going to heaven. I pictured that I would be one of those ghosts rattling around my home, because I wouldn't be able to cut the cosmic umbilical cord. I thought my aching for them all would be so great I could never move on. And I assumed I wouldn't *want* them to move on. Not really. I mean, yes, in some bullshit-piousness sort of way, I might have mouthed it. But I didn't *mean* it. If they all moved on, then they would forget me.

But time has no meaning here. And I'm able to visit them, mostly at night, or when they conjure me. When

Michael's internal conversations with me get really loud in his head, next thing I know, I'm next to his desk, looking at him with his head in his hands. I know he's wondering what to do.

It's not easy to help them. I whisper mostly. I urge them in ways they think is their own mind, but it's not. It's angels. Or whatever we are. I don't have wings. And I don't have high heels. I don't even have form. I just have this whisper.

It was me who told Tara to take pictures. I wander next to her as she walks the fields behind the elementary school near our house, until she feels something and she becomes fascinated by it. For that moment, as she is lining up her perfect shot, lost in a world of gray and black and white—it's as if she *sees* the way the shadows at dusk are going to look in the photo when it's developed—her grief leaves her. She is borne on her art to a place on the other side of grief, a valley that isn't like the place you came from. It's not a happy valley or a place that's idyllic, but after a while you realize you could stay there for a while. It's not like the valley of the shadow of death, the mourning place. It's a resting place as you gather your strength for the future. When she gets to that valley while she's shooting her pictures, I leave. Like magic. I'm somewhere else. In someone else's conversation with me.

Noah calls me the most. I spend a lot of time in his room. My whispers to him aren't about anything. You see, he's young. And I know he's going to be okay with Michael. He'll always ache for me a little bit, but he's going to grow up and find love and have his own kids. Don't ask me how I know, it's just some innate friggin' internal barometer here. And when he has those kids, a part of his heart will shatter again. He won't know why, most likely because he thinks he's always dealt with death and not having me there. But then he'll see bits of me in his kids and bits of him. And at the same time, he'll know he's okay and what a compassionate man he became because he lost me. He'll love his kids more fiercely and harder and with more passion and with more appreciation. He'll never be a workaholic because he doesn't ever want to miss bedtime.

Knowing all this, I don't whisper anything. I sing.

On earth, frankly, I was tone-deaf. All those years singing in the discos with Michael, it was a good thing the volume was up at "ear shatter" because that way no one could hear me singing "I Love the Nightlife." But I always, in private, when my babies were little, or when they were sick, had this aimless mother's tune. "La, la, la, la" followed by a humming. It's not a tune anyone could hum along with—but it was always the same tune. The same exact tune, pitch, everything. And I would sing it and rock my child.

So now I sing it to him, endlessly—me, who always hated Mondays and was never on time…I have nothing but time. So I sing it and hum it over and over and over again. I don't need to sleep here. I'm never tired. I'm never in pain. So I sing it and after a while, he gets a little smile on his face. Then I know he's in the resting valley with Tara. And I vanish to somewhere else.

Pete…he really grieved. Some nights in his room, his face would be covered in tears. Memories of sex permeated, and the way we laughed and held each other. After a while, he moved to the valley, and after that, I saw him with Michael. Then I knew he would be okay. Some time later, I saw him with Michael and a woman who became his girlfriend. She was lovely. Nothing like me. Another teacher. But lovely. You don't feel happiness and sadness here. It's more like this *compassion*. You feel a loving kindness, bare of the intensities of jealousy, anger. You want only good; in fact, you can't do anything that causes harm. So I liked his friend, and I liked how she was to Noah. She would sit next to him and read to him sometimes. One more person to help him. That was good.

Joe.

A tough nut.

More than likely, I would be someplace beautiful, next to a stream, or even basking in white light, and before I knew it, I'd be in his office, door shut and listening to him mutter to himself. He was mad at me for leaving him. Mad at the world. I realized he wasn't going to get to the resting valley, which required a suspension of cynicism. So the best I could do was hope for a dulling of the pain and something new to distract him. When he gets here—years from now as the mean and ornery often live a long time—he'll start to make sense of the whole process.

So one day I found myself in a young woman's room. I had never seen her before. She had a collection of

Fender guitars, a stereo system with reggae blaring and, looking over her shoulder, a way with words.

Next to her was circled an ad for an intern for the *Tribune.* Shitty pay, long hours and no pats on the back, I was certain.

So I talked to her for a week.

Do your résumé.

Send it.

Mail it.

Did you go to the post office yet?

Come on.

Come on.

Now, when he calls you for the interview, don't kiss his ass. He hates that. Show him your spunk.

Great taste in music. How about a little Aretha?

Okay, staying focused, if he gives you a hard time, give him a little bit of a hard time back. Then grin at him to show him you're not afraid of him and that you'll work harder for him than anyone else he's interviewing. Even me.

You're meant to be there.

Next time I visited Joe, this young woman was there. Working hard. Drinking *lots* of coffee.

After that, I didn't visit Joe that often.

Which was a good thing.

George. He didn't really know me. Maybe a year after I left, he called to me.

"Lily…please tell me I'm doing the right thing. Please, Lord. Send me a sign."

It was a prayer, out loud. His apartment was a mess. Boxes piled high. He had sold his restaurant and was moving to the 'burbs. Moving in. Tara was a year away from college. Noah getting taller—I could tell from pictures in frames. And George was crying. I saw contracts on the table—he was buying a small restaurant one town over from my house. But not the Upper East Side. Not the glamour. Not the same clientele. The same renown.

Now, no one ever told me that I couldn't do ghostly things like slam doors. Unfortunately, however, I wouldn't—without form—know how, I don't think. But I started to wonder why I couldn't—hypothetically. It wasn't like there was this great heavenly orientation. And I can tell you St. Peter—Golden Gates—nope.

I thought hard. But no one had said anything.

And if they had…I was never much a rule-follower anyway.

So I looked around George's apartment. The window to the fire escape was open. And outside was one of those pesky New York pigeons. But it was a pretty one. Plump, almost white.

Hey bird. Fly in here for me. Don't get all freaked out. Just come in, land on the contract over here. Coo a few times. Fly out. You're no dove of peace, but you'll have to do.

The bird just blinked.

I coaxed some more.

In fact, the bird and I seemed to be in some sort of stand-off. The bird wasn't coming in. But he seemed paralyzed to fly off.

The sun started to set, and finally…the bird flew in.

George looked up, startled. The bird fluttered to the

dining room table and landed precisely on the contract. George didn't move a muscle. I had to look closely to see if he was even breathing.

The bird stared at George.

George stared at the bird.

The bird cooed.

Then off it flew.

George smiled. He wiped at his face, and then he let out this whoop of a laugh.

And I was whisked away.

Frankly, I was tired of being at everyone's beck and call. Not tired in a crabby Earth way, but it seemed like every time I was someplace so perfect and beautiful and peaceful, I was sent somewhere else.

After I had been gone a while, after George moved in, I was called to Michael. He was in a church. Whispering. I looked around. Ash Wednesday. Could tell by the grayish cross smeared on his forehead.

"I feel so lost."

I was next to him in the pew.

Remember the time we went to the Jersey Shore and stayed at that seedy motel because we were both broke and it was all we could afford? We drove down in that piece of crap you drove—with the smashed-in taillight.

We even brought our own rotgut vodka because we knew we couldn't afford a motel room, McDonald's and to go out to the clubs. Remember?

We went down to the beach at night. Sat on the sand, lights from the boardwalk in back of us. And out of nowhere—and you were pretty drunk—you kissed me.

I was shocked. And I guess the vodka had gone to our heads. We were kissing. I remember you slipped a hand down to my breast. My right breast. Man, I have a memory here.

And then I pulled back and looked at you. And we both stopped. We didn't say a word. We just stopped.

For about ten minutes, we both faced the ocean and watched the waves roll in. Jersey Shore wind whipped us. Kind of cold, even for July. Blowing sand bit my face.

We didn't say anything. I don't know what you were thinking. I know what I was thinking.

So I spoke, out loud, into the wind.

"You know, we'd just ruin it. Someday, this friendship is going to mean more to us than sex. More than almost anything in our lives. We'll have a permanence that transcends boyfriends, and bad dates, and burning down apartments, and bad cooking, and bad vodka, and everything else. Because you are you, and I am me, we get to transcend it all. Isn't that special, Michael?"

And you just smiled.

And I remember that night, later, you in your creaky twin bed with the moldy bedspread and me in mine, you told me about the assault. And you said, "Lily…you're my best friend. You're the first friend I've had since then. And right now, you're the only friend I need."

And then you rolled over and went to sleep.

I looked over at Michael. He was smiling. And next thing I knew I was swept away.

Time went by and I was swept to my friends and family less and less. Michael completed his novel. He made peace with the horror of his team's betrayal. George's new restaurant was a success. My children smiled more. I became used to my peace and my serenity here. My compassion became focused less and less on them— though I always loved them best—and more and more on the world as a whole.

Every once in a while, I crave a martini. And I'm swept back for a few minutes. There they all are talking about me around the dinner table. They look different. My kids are older. Tara's in college. But they talk about me not in the resting valley, not in a stopping place of grief, but in a good place. So I only get to glimpse them for a minute—and it's bittersweet, not the stabbing grief. I think it's God's way of letting this side know it's okay. And letting that side still feel us until they come join us.

Bad things do happen to good people. People get cancer. They hurt each other. They say things that they wish they could take back but can't.

And when I got here, I thought I'd have all the answers. But the funny thing is, I learned that I had the answer all along.

Just love them.

Just love them all.

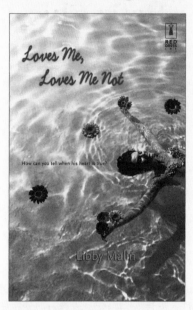